IN SUMMER LIGHT

ALSO BY ZIBBY ONEAL

The Language of Goldfish
A Formal Feeling

ZIBBY ONEAL

IN
SUMMER
LIGHT

VIKING KESTREL

VIKING KESTREL

Viking Penguin Inc., 40 West 23rd Street, New York, New York 10010, U.S.A.
Penguin Books Ltd, Harmondsworth, Middlesex, England
Penguin Books Australia Ltd, Ringwood, Victoria, Australia
Penguin Books Canada Limited, 2801 John Street, Markham, Ontario, Canada L3R 1B4
Penguin Books (N.Z.) Ltd, 182–190 Wairau Road, Auckland 10, New Zealand

First published in 1985 by Viking Penguin Inc.
Published simultaneously in Canada

Printed in the United States of America by
The Book Press, Brattleboro, Vermont
Set in Sabon Roman
3   4   5   89   88   87   86

Library of Congress Cataloging in Publication Data
Oneal, Zibby.   In summer light.
Summary: With the help of an attractive graduate student,
Kate endures a summer with her overpowering artist father
and gains the courage to pursue her own artistic goals.
[1. Artists—Fiction] I. Title.
PZ7.O552Ip   1985   [Fic]   85-50806   ISBN 0-670-80784-2

TO DEBORAH BRODIE

IN SUMMER LIGHT

C H A P T E R

1

There were peaches in a blue and white Chinese bowl and a cat almost the color of peaches stretched beneath the table. Morning light fell slantwise across the table's surface, lay like marmalade on the rungs of a ladder-back chair. Beside the table, sitting straight on the straight-backed chair, was a little girl, feet bare, hands folded. Her dark hair grazed the sharp bones of her shoulders. Her eyes were intent. Perched there expectantly, erect on the chair's edge, she was like someone awaiting an invitation to dance.

The painting hung above the mantelpiece in the narrow farmhouse sitting room. Passing it on this rainy morning, dangling an empty coffee cup from the crook of her thumb, Kate paused and glanced up at it. She had been ten when she posed for the painting. Now she was seventeen.

In its heavy gilded frame, it seemed at odds with the other paintings in the room. These others—squalls of color, whirling shapes—were entirely abstract. They comprised what critics referred to as Marcus Brewer's later style, meaning the style for which Kate's father was famous.

Kate yawned. She'd seen a reproduction once in a book at school. Leah had found it in the library and brought it back to the room they shared, and they'd looked at the child and the chair and the cat in the painting's middle distance, and at the scrawled signature occupying its foreground, and Leah had said, "He should have called the painting 'Kate.' " Kate recalled laughing.

She almost laughed now, but then she yawned again and remembered she'd come downstairs for coffee.

The rain that had been lashing the house all morning streamed down the kitchen windows. It was the kind of violent three-day rain that often swept the island in June, blowing in across the Sound from the coast of Massachusetts. Kate poured herself coffee and leaned against the sink. "There'll be a lot of unhappy day-trippers on the ferries today," she said.

"Wouldn't you think they'd wait for the weather to clear?" said her mother.

"Yes, but they don't. They never do." And Kate had a sudden vision of crowds of sodden and disgruntled tourists wandering the streets in town.

Her mother was standing at the kitchen table, arranging nasturtiums in the Chinese bowl. When she had finished, she would put the bowl on the mantelpiece below the painted one because it amused Kate's father to see it there—the illusion above the reality. Away at school, Kate forgot such details, and there were dozens of them. The house was full of these small gestures designed to please her father.

Her mother stood back and frowned at the bowl. "That's pretty," Kate said, "You're good with color."

"Not especially. It was your father who chose the color. I'm imitating."

"Nasturtiums are *not* the same color as peaches," Kate said. And, of course, they weren't. There was a pale gold in the skin of a peach, a suggestion of the flesh beneath, that was entirely lacking in the flowers. Her mother had created something different, but Kate knew it was pointless to insist. She sipped her coffee.

"How are you feeling?" her mother said.

"Tired."

"Already?"

"It comes and goes."

And that was true. That was apparently typical of mononucleosis, or so she'd been told in the infirmary. At just those moments when she thought she was better her fever rose again, the glands in her neck began to ache, and she felt the heavy pull of fatigue, dragging her back into lethargy. It had been that way since May. They had told her that it could last six weeks longer. Consequently she was home for the summer, and tired, and when she was not too tired, bored.

"I dreamed I was on Long Island," she said. "Leah and I had jobs, just the way we'd planned."

"Poor Kate. Maybe you can go down for a visit when you're well."

"No, I can't. Leah *does* have a job. She isn't going to want me hanging around doing nothing."

Her mother sighed and brushed back her hair. It was long and dark like Kate's. She was barefoot, too—tan legs beneath a loose dress of Mexican cotton. Both of them were tall, both slender. The difference lay in their faces. Kate's was like her father's—narrow and restless. She had his high cheekbones and black eyes, and an impatience about her mouth that was also his. When it came to faces, it was her sister, Amanda, who looked like her mother.

Kate leaned over and slopped the rest of her coffee into the sink. "I guess what I ought to do is go back upstairs and work on my paper," she said.

"How's it coming?"

Kate shrugged. The truth was that it wasn't coming much better than it had the last few weeks of school when she had felt too sick to work on it. "I guess the answer is slowly," she said. "The thing is, I don't like *The Tempest.*"

"You like Shakespeare," her mother said, saying it as if she were speaking of a slightly exotic taste.

"That's beside the point, Mother. It's not Shakespeare, it's this play. Naturally I like Shakespeare. *Everyone* likes Shakespeare. Even Amanda likes him. I read her a couple of Ariel's songs. She thinks they're 'cool.' "

"Do you suppose she'll want to be an English major, too?"

"Hard to tell about a seven-year-old, wouldn't you say?"

But something in her mother's tone made Kate defensive. "Do you *mind* that I may want to major in English?" she said. "You always sound disappointed."

"No. I'm just used to artists."

"You're used to *an* artist," Kate said.

"Well, not quite. I've spent most of my life around them one way or another. I suppose I assumed you'd be one, too. When I think of all the years you spent painting—"

"I haven't painted in quite awhile," Kate said.

Her mother said, "I know."

In the silence that followed, her mother stooped to scoop up Amanda's sandals from beside the stove. Kate listened to the rain. The kitchen where they stood was old-fashioned, unremodeled—a farmhouse kitchen that had once appeared on the cover of a national magazine, background to a photograph of Kate's father. Today it was dim in the gray-green storm light.

"You know why I don't like *The Tempest?*" Kate said. "It's because of Prospero. He reminds me of Father."

"Don't start that, Kate."

"I'm not starting anything. I'm just telling you why I don't like *The Tempest.*"

Her mother dropped Amanda's sandals on the table. "I wish you could try to get along with him this summer," she said.

"I can't," Kate said simply, and then to forestall further discussion, she crossed the kitchen and leaned against the screen door, looking out at the rain.

The discussion was like an old piece of knitting, raveled

and knitted and raveled again until the thread almost fell into place by itself. It had been several years since she'd gotten along with her father. If she ever had. If "getting along" had ever been more than an illusion. The irony was that the only person who noticed or cared was her mother. Her father wouldn't have known what they meant.

She stood looking out at the rainswept meadow, and at the studio that seemed to float in its center, aloof on swells of green. Down there he was painting, he and his canvas making an island together on this larger island where the rest of them lived.

Well, the hell with him, she thought, and turned and saw through the window that there was a car hesitating at the end of the driveway. It was some kind of old, no-color car that looked as if it had been driven to the point of collapse. As Kate watched, it turned and began to pull in. "Somebody coming," she said.

Her mother looked up.

"Someone with a California license plate, if you can believe that."

"Oh, Lord, it's that graduate student," her mother said. "I thought he'd take an afternoon boat."

"What graduate student?" Dimly Kate remembered some mention of this, but she'd paid no attention. There were always people arriving to see her father—critics, interviewers, professors from various universities. Once a whole television crew had come to make a documentary. Week after week people came and went, although the house was intentionally inaccessible, and the island was a seven-mile ferry ride from the mainland.

"He's the one who's coming to do the cataloging for the exhibit in Berkeley," her mother said. "What in the world will I give him for lunch?"

The car edged up to the side of the house, stopped, trembled, and continued to tremble even after the motor shut off. The door opened. A tall figure in a yellow slicker ducked out and came running across the grass, bent against the rain. "He's going to the front door," Kate said. "Wouldn't you think in a monsoon he might choose the closest one?"

She knew immediately the type he'd be—polite, in awe, much too much in awe of the great painter to use anything but the front door. No surprises there, she thought, and went to let him in.

He stood on the porch, about to ring, wet as the survivor of a shipwreck. "I don't know if I'm in the right place," he said. "I'm looking for Marcus Brewer's house."

Kate pushed open the screen door. "You've found it," she said. "I'm Kate."

2

"Painting," her father said, "is like making love."

Kate glanced up sharply. He was really going full steam tonight, she thought.

Around the table, forks clicked against plates. A damp-smelling breeze coming through the open windows stirred the curtains. Bluefish, peas from the garden, and her father announcing that painting was like making love. A normal family dinner. Kate wondered what this graduate student—this Ian Jackson—thought.

At one time her father's saying this would have embarrassed her. Now she was merely annoyed. Like his hands, flying every which way, painting the air as he talked, the statement's extravagance struck her as ridiculous. She supposed it was for Ian Jackson's benefit, since the rest of them had heard him say it before.

10

"Making lanyards is like braiding hair," said Amanda. "Sort of."

Having shoved her bluefish around her plate long enough to satisfy their mother, Amanda was now tracing patterns in spilled salt. "We learned how in day camp," she said. "It's easy." And then she turned conversationally to Ian Jackson. "Did you know Kate has mono?" she said.

For some reason this fact fascinated Amanda. She liked telling people. She liked the word, and especially its abbreviation. Ian Jackson started to reply.

"Nobody ever heard of such a disease in my day," their father said. "At least they never gave it a name that I know of."

Kate rested her fork on her plate. "There were twenty-three cases at school this year," she said.

"Give something a name and you create an epidemic," said her father.

"There *was* a kind of epidemic at Berkeley this year," Ian Jackson said. Then he smiled at Kate. "I've heard you feel pretty awful the first few weeks."

Kate looked at him thoughtfully. "You do," she said.

She guessed that he might be twenty-four or five. Red-haired and very tall, he would in other circumstances have seemed enormous, but, beside her father, no one seemed enormous. Beside her father, people dwindled.

It was her father's energy that did it. He was white-haired and sixty years old—nearly twelve years older than her mother—but, sitting at the end of the table, he seemed no age at all. He was barely contained in his chair. Moving, shifting, his hands describing circles in the air, he made a magnetic field of the space around him.

"If you want to talk about epidemics," he said, "take Abstract Expressionism. *There* was an epidemic for you. They came up with a name and suddenly there were Abstract Expressionists coming out of the woodwork." He flung out his arm, nearly upsetting his wine glass. "Anyone in those days was suddenly an artist."

"I suppose because it was harder to see any obvious discipline in those paintings," Ian said.

"Damned right! Of course. They look slapdash if you don't know better. People began to think anyone could dribble some paint up and down a canvas. There were artists all over New York doing that those years. In fact, when I met Floss she was doing one. Remember that big thing, Floss? What did you call it? 'Coney Island'?"

Kate's mother paused, serving a spoonful of peas. " 'Jones Beach,' " she said.

"Oh, right. Well, I knew it had the name of some swimming place."

Even Amanda would know the name of that painting, Kate thought. It was the only one of the, presumably, many her mother had painted in the years when she *did* paint that she'd kept. It was stored in the attic, wrapped in sheets. Kate had seen it there often.

"You paint, Mrs. Brewer?" Ian said.

"She used to. When I met her, she was painting."

Kate looked at her mother. "Years ago I did," her mother said. "For a little while."

12

"For fifteen years, in fact," Kate amended.

"She painted a mural on my wall," said Amanda. "I told her what to put in, so there's a skunk and a clown and a lot of stuff. If you want, I can show you after dinner."

"As you see," their father said to Ian, "in a painter's family everyone gets into the act."

"Not Kate," said Amanda.

There were strawberries for dessert. Kate set the bowl on the table before her mother and handed dishes around as her mother filled them. The talk went on. Late sunlight slanted in through the windows and across the glossy yellow pine of the table. Amanda quietly smoothed the salt.

"So do you want to?" she said suddenly to Ian. "Do you want to see the mural my mother painted?"

"Ian doesn't want to see your mural, baby," their father said. "He's hardly seen anything around the place yet."

"I've seen some of the paintings," Ian said. "Mrs. Brewer showed me the ones in the house."

"Floss remembers more about them than I do. But you ought to take a look around outside now that the rain's stopped."

"Show him the pond," Amanda said. "That's the best part. It's full of leeches."

"Not overwhelmingly full," said their father. "You want to show him, Kate?"

The rain had stopped before dinner, but the grass was still wet. Kate led the way, pushing through the tall grass, shaking down small showers. "By the middle of the summer, there'll be a path worn through here," she said. "It vanishes year to year and we have to tramp it down again. Other people mow their meadows, but my mother likes to give the wildflowers a chance." She glanced over her shoulder at Ian making his way through the grass behind her. "Do you recognize poison ivy?" she said.

He shook his head. "Not poison ivy or leeches. I don't know if we have such things in California."

"Well, look," Kate paused and pointed to a patch growing low to the ground. "That's it. In a few weeks, it will be all over the meadow. Watch out for it when you come down swimming."

"And leeches?"

"Oh, that's just Amanda. She's dramatic."

They walked on in silence. Kate could hear the swish of the grass behind her. The air smelled sweet after the rain, smelled of the wild roses that bloomed in the meadow in great tangled thickets of old cane. "You must like living here," Ian said.

"I'm not here much—just summers and Christmas. I go to school in Connecticut."

"College?"

She was surprised he thought so. "Boarding school," she said. "I'll be a senior."

"I should have known that."

"Why?"

"Well, I've read so much about your father."

"Oh, right." Kate switched at the grass with her hand. "Articles where his family is cataloged with reference to dates same as his paintings."

14

Ian laughed. "I guess it must be hard sometimes, being his family."

Kate glanced back at him. "We manage."

It had sounded like the kind of curiosity she was used to. All the visitors seemed to have it. They wanted souvenirs—little bits of information they could put in their pockets and take home. She could imagine him next winter in Berkeley, pulling out his souvenir, telling his friends that Marcus Brewer's daughter had admitted it wasn't so easy being that, unpacking the information like an interesting shell he'd discovered in the sand.

"The pond is just past the stone wall," she said. "Just there beyond the elder bushes. It's a good place to swim if you haven't time to go to the beach. On the other side is a salt marsh. My father owns that, too."

"It's pretty," Ian said. "It's a gentle sort of landscape." And then, "What are the yellow flowers?"

"You'd have to ask my mother."

"They're nice with the roses."

"I know. The colors in the meadow this time of year remind me of a Bonnard."

"You aren't a painter?"

"God, no."

"But you think about colors."

"I don't much. I notice them. If you live in this family, you notice them. But contrary to what my father said, we don't all get into the act. As a matter of fact, none of us do anymore." She pulled a stem of grass and twirled it in her fingers. "I'm going to major in English in college."

"Your own field to plow," said Ian.

"My what?"

"You want to do your own thing."

Kate looked at him, startled. "Well, yes," she said. "I do."

It was what she had tried explaining more than once to her mother. She was surprised that he understood so easily.

"How long are you going to be here?" she said.

"Can't be sure yet. I don't know how much will be involved. A month. Six weeks."

"That long? Just to list some paintings?"

He laughed. "There's more to cataloging than that, especially for a big retrospective show like this one," he said. "Come around one day and I'll show you."

She left him at the door of the little back room in the studio where he would stay while he was there. Then she walked back to the house. Amanda was sitting on the porch steps, braiding. Kate slumped down beside her and leaned against the flaking pillar of the porch.

"Feeling funny again?" said Amanda.

"Moderately."

She could feel that her temperature had risen a little, just enough to make her gently light-headed. It wasn't uncomfortable; in fact it was pleasant to feel slightly disconnected. She closed her eyes and watched colors skate beneath her lids like water skimmers on the pond.

"I like him," Amanda said. "Do you?"

"Hard to tell yet."

"Not for me. I could tell right away. He isn't like most

16

of them who don't talk to kids. I'm probably going to teach him to braid lanyards."

Kate looked out across the meadow, lit now with the last rays of watery evening sunlight. Her own field to plow. It was a funny way to put it, but she liked it. It was exact. It would be a field quite different from the meadow—that overgrown tangle of grass and wildflowers that, for all its size, seemed forever dwarfed by the studio. Hers would be a neat field, carefully planned. Most of all, it would be her own.

She leaned forward and picked at a splinter of wood, still soft from the rain. It would be like her half of the room at school, as neat as Leah's was chaotic, almost bare in fact, and monotone. A cell, that's what Leah said it looked like. But it suited Kate. She had never bothered trying to explain to Leah that she had had enough of color.

3

Her room at home was something else entirely. Here, noth-ing that had accumulated had ever been thrown away. Her old stuffed rabbit still sat on the bookshelf. Childhood watercolors fluttered on the pegboard on the wall. Added to these were posters and books, tapes and records, snapshots of friends, a hockey stick. And the desk. Who could remember what had been stuffed into the desk drawers in the seven years that Kate had occupied this room?

Waking, she looked about her thoughtfully and with distaste, remembering her perfectly orderly space at school. This room was like every other one in the house, carelessly, casually stuffed with things that no one thought to discard. It made her uncomfortable that this should be true, as if the house were sucking her in, engulfing her again in its disorder. She began stripping the room in her mind's eye, packing up the posters, the watercolors, the rabbit, until in her imagination she had a pure rectangle of white plaster, a few books stacked neatly on the desk, perhaps curtains. With an energy she hadn't felt in weeks, Kate shoved back the covers and got up, thinking that she would start the project at once.

It wasn't early. She could tell by the angle of light on the floor that it was after nine o'clock. And, judging by the sounds in the house, Mrs. Hilmer had arrived and was cleaning, trying, as she did three times a week, to make some order out of what Kate's mother never got around to. Kate pulled a ragged robe from a hook in the closet. She would like very much to avoid talking to Mrs. Hilmer, she thought, but she would also very much like some breakfast. She didn't see how she could manage one without the other.

As often as not, Mrs. Hilmer brought along her daughter, Frances, who was ten. She reminded Kate of a toadstool, always hanging around in some corner as if she'd grown there, as if, in fact, she owned the space. Kate opened the door of her bedroom cautiously, half-expecting Frances to be planted on the other side. Then she tiptoed down the hall to the bathroom and brushed her teeth.

From the top of the stairs, she could see Mrs. Hilmer in the sitting room, dusting the mantel as if she were aiming to wipe out some disease, which was the way she cleaned everything. Kate started down the stairs, leaning on the bannister to prevent creaking. But the stairs creaked anyway, and Mrs. Hilmer turned.

"No worms for you," she said.

Kate stopped and looked at her.

"Worms are for the early birds," Mrs. Hilmer said, and went back to dusting.

"Oh, right." Kate came the rest of the way downstairs.

In the kitchen she looked around for coffee. "I washed the pot," Mrs. Hilmer called.

"Well, but we'll have to make more to take down to the studio, so I might as well do it now."

"Your mother said you were to take him his thermos. She's gone to town to teach her class."

Twice a week her mother taught a children's painting class at the library in town. Kate picked up the empty pot and carried it to the sitting room door. "When will she be home?"

Mrs. Hilmer shrugged. "Not before it's time to take down his coffee." And then, "You don't look much like your picture here anymore," as if this thought followed directly on the other.

Kate glanced at the painting. "Well, I was ten there."

"Same age as my Frances."

Kate nodded.

"I'd like a nice oil painting of her," Mrs. Hilmer said. "I told your mother I'd work it off if he'd paint it."

"My father?"

"Who else would I mean?"

"But he doesn't do portraits."

"That's what your mother said. But I don't know what you'd call this if it isn't a portrait."

"It's a kind of study," Kate said. "It's a—" She shrugged. "It's an exploration of light." She looked up at the picture. "Don't you see how the cat is kind of dissolving around the edges? How it's more just color than cat?"

Mrs. Hilmer laid down her dustcloth and squinted up at the painting. The cat, the chair, the child—all dissolving in the painting's light. Kate wondered whether Mrs. Hilmer could see or understand this.

"Don't you see, Mrs. Hilmer? The objects don't really matter here. They could be anything—grapes and bottles."

"I don't see how. If it was grapes and bottles, it wouldn't be a picture of you."

"It isn't a picture of me," Kate said.

"Looks that way to me," said Mrs. Hilmer, and Kate only nodded, because of course it had looked that way to her, too, once. Until she had begun to see what it was really meant to be, she had thought the painting was her portrait.

She could remember clearly the day she discovered that this was not so. She had heard him talking to a visitor, standing beneath the painting as Mrs. Hilmer now stood. "If you look closely at the cat," he'd said, "or at the chair, or at the figure on the chair, you can see that, as objects, they don't really matter. They are only colors occupying space."

This had baffled Kate. She hadn't guessed that in the hours she posed for him she was only a color filling space. In fact, she had imagined that, when he had finished, he would call the painting "Kate." He had called it "The Studio: Morning."

But no point trying to explain all this to Mrs. Hilmer.

21

Instead, Kate went back into the kitchen, filled the coffee pot with water, measured out coffee and plugged in the pot. Mrs. Hilmer's voice trailed her. "Frances could wear her Easter dress," she called. Kate didn't answer.

He had never done real portraits, she supposed, but there had been a time when his paintings contained figures and faces and objects drawn from a recognizable world. It was only after they moved to the island that his pictures had begun to change. The real world had stopped mattering, and bit by bit it had disappeared from his canvases, replaced by shape and color alone. Self-portraits, Kate thought. That's what they had become—paintings of the contents of his mind.

She found the old, gray, dented thermos her mother had used for years to carry his coffee to the studio every morning precisely at ten. She set it on the kitchen table, and, while the coffee was brewing, went back upstairs to dress.

Kate rarely went to the studio now, and never except on errands. Once she had been there nearly every day, sprawled on the floor beside him with her watercolors, or later, when she was older, painting at a table of her own. Long ago, Kate thought. History.

She could remember hurrying home from grade school to paint, and long summer afternoons when nothing interrupted them at work. He always outlasted her. Sometimes, finally tired of painting, she would gather up her things and wait for him outside the studio. Half-concealed in the tall grass, she would listen for the warning squeak of the screen door, ready to jump up and tag after him

22

when he appeared. She had dozens of questions to ask, saved up over the hours of keeping silent in the studio. Cobalt blue—what was cobalt? And burnt umber—was it really burned? She had memorized the names on his tubes of paint. She ran after him, trying to keep up with his long strides, asking questions, wanting to know.

And what for? What had been the use of any of that as it turned out?

At the door of the studio Kate paused, balancing the thermos on her hip. Through the screen she could see her father, standing back from the easel to survey whatever it was he was working on. She knocked twice before he heard her. "Coffee," she said. He motioned her in.

"Can you just put it there on the table?" he said, and Kate crossed the room and put the thermos on the table among the clutter of paint tubes.

On the easel was a large canvas. He never painted small canvases now, as if nothing but these enormous expanses were enough to hold what he imagined. Across its center ran a dark line, frail as spiderweb. The line cut across a rumple of yellow—many shades of yellow, thickly applied and closely graded, tangled like sheets on an unmade bed. Kate glanced quickly, and then looked more thoughtfully. There was something wrong with it.

"What do you think?" he said, nodding at the canvas.

Kate didn't answer.

"Well?"

"It's nice," she said, and wondered whether he'd know she was lying.

"Nice?" he said.

"Well, interesting."

"Actually," he said, "it's a mess. I've been looking at it all morning and I can't see a damned thing that's going right with it."

"I'm probably the wrong person to give an opinion," Kate said, "since I'm not a painter."

"Well, even if you were," he said, and his voice trailed off, not finishing the thought. He stared at the canvas.

Kate recognized the look in his eyes. She had seen it often before, this intensity, this energy, engaged in a struggle with the canvas. It might have been only a week ago that she sat tense on the edge of her chair, thinking that this was what it meant to be a painter—this struggling, this slow rhythm of looking and moving, this intense dance.

He moved beside her now, but it was only a shift of position. "It seems to get harder all the time," he said. "There must be some kind of joke in that." And then, running his hand through his hair, he seemed slowly to change focus. "Are you feeling any better?" he asked.

"Part of the time."

"Your mother says you have some work to catch up on. She says you're writing a big critical paper about something or other."

"About *The Tempest*," Kate said. "For English. This year we studied Shakespeare." But she knew he wasn't listening. The painting was like a third person in the room, claiming his attention. His eyes traveled back to it irresistibly, as they might have to someone well loved. And

24

Kate, without bothering to say she was going, turned and started for the door.

She didn't think he'd noticed her going, but when she was about to open the screen, he turned toward her, vague-eyed. "I never did think much of criticism," he said absently. "In my opinion, dead from the waist down."

Kate shut the door. She knew what he meant. He hadn't been thinking about her paper, but about the articles that occasionally appeared that didn't praise his work. He hadn't meant to hurt her. It hadn't occurred to him that he might.

But why shouldn't it occur to him, she thought, and slapped at a weed beside the path. Why was he the only one of them who didn't have to think of things like that?

By the time she had reached the house again, she felt too tired to start on her room. Instead she decided to work on the paper. A solid project, firmly her own. With the vacuum for accompaniment, she read, marking Mrs. Hilmer's progress through the downstairs room by the greater or lesser roar of the motor.

She would have preferred almost any other play. *Hamlet. Macbeth.* Any of them. She had hated being assigned *The Tempest,* though at first she hadn't known why. All spring she and Leah argued about the play, over and over, sitting cross-legged on their beds at school. Leah's version of Prospero as a darling, white-haired old magician was not one that Kate shared.

"What's so darling about him?" Kate had asked. "He uses everyone. They run around doing whatever it is he wants and he doesn't give a damn how they feel."

"But he means well, Kate. He's good to Miranda."

"Is that right? 'I have done nothing but in care of thee, my daughter'? If you believe that, Leah, you're crazy. Think about it awhile."

"Well, but Kate, he's a wizard!"

"So?"

"So, that's like being a genius. You have to make allowances."

And it was then that Kate had begun to see how much Prospero reminded her of her father. They'd all been making allowances for him for years. Because he was a genius.

Now, sitting at her desk, she looked out her window, wondering if there might be a way to leave Prospero out of the paper entirely. Below her the vacuum roared toward the stairway. Kate smiled. No way she could think of, unless she wanted an F on the paper.

Through the window, she could see Ian coming up the path from the studio. When he reached the apron of mowed grass behind the house, he turned toward the barn that served as a garage. He walked like a westerner, Kate thought, moving with long, loose strides that seemed to take for granted that there was abundant space for moving. She watched him enter the barn. In another minute she heard the coughing of his old car, and then saw the car itself, inching backward down the gravel driveway. She sighed and looked again at the page she was reading. When she looked up again, the car was gone.

And suddenly the house was quiet. The vacuum had fallen silent. Mrs. Hilmer was through for the day, having

26

given up temporarily on her struggle with clutter. Kate could hear Ian's car start up the rise in the road beyond the house, and then that sound, too, died away. The stillness was distracting. She had learned, at school, to concentrate in spite of noise, and now she couldn't concentrate without it. She stood up and pushed back the chair and went to look for an old tape recorder that she thought might still be stored in her closet.

Might be? Of course it would be stored there, together with the rest of the jumble that represented years of stuffing things away.

She tugged at the things on the closet floor, pulling out a box of old sweaters, a Frisbee, her school yearbooks in a stack. She saw the tape recorder at last, lying behind a pile of children's books. And behind it she saw the painting.

It was wrapped in bath towels, propped against the closet wall. There was dust along the top edge of the towel—a two and a half year accumulation. Taped to the back of the canvas was the ribbon the painting had won. Kate knew this because she had taped it there herself before wrapping the picture and putting it away. Seeing it now, she had no wish to unwrap it. That was all over. But she did think, before she pulled out the tape recorder and closed the closet door, how like "Jones Beach" it was, resting in the closet, neatly wrapped and tucked away where it wouldn't bother anyone.

4

After the three-day spell of rain, the weather was perfect.
Day after day passed hot and cloudless. In the meadow
the tiger lilies began to bloom earlier than they did most
years, their orange blossoms swaying above clouds of
daisies. Kate's mother gathered them for the house, going
down into the meadow early in the morning when the
flowers were just opening and returning with armloads.

Kate watched her do this, baffled. They were *day* lilies
she gathered. The flowers didn't last until dinner. But she
returned from the meadow, the hem of her skirt wet, her
blouse smeared with pollen, carrying her armloads as gently
as she would a sleeping child.

And then she arranged them. Arranged them! These
flowers that lasted less than a day. She gave as much care
to arranging them as she might have given to a permanent

work of art. And why? Because Kate's father liked them.

"Why don't you at least pick daisies?" Kate said. "That way, a few flowers would still be open by five o'clock."

Her mother settled the lilies on the kitchen table. "Some of these buds will open tomorrow," she said.

Kate tipped back on the kitchen chair, balancing herself on the back legs. The futility of all this made her impatient. It was like so much else she didn't understand about her mother, whose life seemed like a patchwork, stitched together without plan or center. Flowers, guests, teaching small children to finger paint. Parts but no whole.

"Mrs. Hilmer wants a portrait of Frances," she said. "I guess you know that."

"Poor Frances," her mother said.

"Why 'poor'?"

"Oh, Mrs. Hilmer is bringing her up like royalty. It's silly, knowing Frances."

"Well, anyway," Kate said, rocking on the chair, "she wants a painting."

Her mother picked up the ironstone pitcher she had filled with flowers and set it on the windowsill. "I told her there were lots of sidewalk painters in town this summer."

"She doesn't want a sidewalk painter. You know that."

Her mother glanced at her. Then she laughed. "I know. You see what I mean about Mrs. Hilmer? Nothing's out of the question for Frances."

"Well, why shouldn't he do it?"

"Don't be silly."

"Why is that silly? What's so sacred about his time that

29

he can't take a little of it to do something for someone else?"

"You're arguing for the sake of arguing," her mother said, which was, of course, true. Hadn't Kate explained the whole thing to Mrs. Hilmer herself? Still, she went on.

"She said she'd work it off. You'd probably get five years of cleaning free."

"Kate, stop it. Your father is one of the most important painters in the country. He isn't going to paint Frances Hilmer."

Kate rocked forward, banging the chair's front legs on the floor. Her mother *had* to say this. The importance of Marcus Brewer, the importance of his work—it was a kind of refrain that ran stated or unstated through everything she said.

"Why don't you do a portrait of Frances then?" she said.

"That's sillier still. I haven't painted in twenty years."

"But you could."

"So could you."

Kate tipped back in the chair and shook her head. They had reached a dead end.

Later Kate lay stretched in a canvas beach chair, watching Amanda and a friend from day camp knocking croquet balls around the lawn. It was a hot afternoon. The air was still, exaggerating the wooden thud of the mallets.

Kate was restless. It was strange to have to be so inactive.

She felt as if she were losing focus, melting in the summer heat, dissolving into a shape without contours.

She had a sense that the separateness she had carved out for herself at school was gradually eroding. It no longer seemed quite so odd that the Chinese bowl was kept on the mantel, that coffee was carried to the studio precisely at ten, that her mother should spend an hour arranging flowers that didn't last a day. Kate felt as if the years she'd been away had contracted to nothing, and she was a child again in this world arranged to please her father.

She sat up and fumbled on the grass beside her for Leah's letter. She'd read it once already. She read it again. It was written on two sides of a yellow legal sheet in headlong script that seemed about to leave the page. Leah was in love. Her job was terrific. The shop gave employees discounts, and she'd already spent her first month's pay on clothes. She'd bought a terrific fuchsia bikini. It had cost a fortune, but so what? Sean liked it. That was his name, Sean. It sounded Irish, but he wasn't.

Kate smiled. Leah wrote the way she talked, breathlessly leaping from one thought to the next, and expecting to be followed. Each time a letter came, Kate missed her, though at the same time the thought of Leah wore her out.

She leaned back in the canvas chair and looked at the green branches above her. She ought to write Leah. She had nothing to say. It had been hot on the island for several days. She wasn't getting much work done. The family seemed about the same. Kate frowned. Utterly boring.

Entirely true.

Suddenly she realized how sick she was of being sick, and how bored, and how lonely. She imagined Leah lying on a beach in her fuchsia bikini, and felt as though she herself had become a blob, like one of the ugly shapeless slugs that live on the underside of broccoli leaves.

The croquet balls clunked. Kate turned her head and squinted down through the meadow. It was hot even in the shade. She pushed herself up out of the chair and decided to go swimming.

Poison ivy had begun to climb the stone wall at the bottom of the meadow. Kate eased herself gingerly over the stones. She could see the edge of the pond through the elder bushes, as still and brown as liquid in a teacup. The flat pads of water lilies floated on the surface. The air smelled brackish. There was a towel on the grass bank, and, coming around the bushes, Kate saw that Ian was floating in the water at the far edge.

She hesitated. He waved, paddling backwards. Kate dropped her towel on the grass and sat down to untie her sneakers.

She rarely saw him during the day. Sometimes, passing the studio, she could hear the pecking of his typewriter through the open windows of his little back room. She had some vague idea of how he spent his days from the conversations she heard at dinner. He seemed a part of the household and not a part which, Kate thought, was intentional. He was careful about intruding. He teased Amanda. He asked Kate about her work. But since the first day when she had shown him the pond, they hadn't had a real conversation.

She left her sneakers beside her towel and waded into the pond. It was lukewarm. The bottom was soft with decaying leaves. A dragonfly hovering above the lily pads darted away as Kate slid into the water. She paddled slowly toward the center, then turned over and floated, steering between lily clumps. She felt weightless, almost disembodied. There was so little difference between the temperature of the water and the temperature of the air that it was hard to tell where her body broke the surface.

She turned her head slightly and looked at Ian. "It's like bathwater," she said.

"But nice."

It was. She closed her eyes and floated silently. The whirring of the dragonflies was the only sound in the still air.

After a while Ian said, "I've been lying here thinking that if I knew how to paint, I'd paint that sky. God, it's beautiful."

It was peacefully, cloudlessly blue. Cobalt, Kate thought. Cerulean. Actually it was both, and twenty other shades as well, not all of them blue.

"Skies are hard to paint," she said. "It has something to do with transparency." She squinted up at the perfect curve above her. "Even watercolor doesn't seem transparent enough to me. I used to paint my skies with plain water."

"I thought you didn't paint."

"I used to. I quit."

A dragonfly whizzed over her like a tiny helicopter looking for a place to touch down. "We've all painted at one time or another."

"I guess it would be hard not to."

Kate looked up at the dragonfly hovering against the sky. "That's what everyone says," she answered.

"How long did you paint?"

"Up until a couple of years ago, as a matter of fact. Up until the middle of my freshman year."

"And then you quit? Why? No time?"

Kate stirred the water with her hands, gently propelling herself away from a stringy clump of water lilies. "No. I don't know. I won a prize for a painting and, after that, it just seemed like a good idea to quit."

"I think I've lost the logic."

"I know. It didn't really have to do with logic. It was more just a feeling."

"It sounds like you were painting fairly seriously."

"Yes," Kate said. "I guess I was."

"Oil?"

"That's right. It was a painting of the meadow that won the prize. I did it from memory, in art class. It was only the second or third oil I'd done, so I didn't expect much."

"And you won. That must have pleased your father."

Kate turned her head to look at him. She smoothed the water with the palms of her hands. "Oh," she said, "not especially."

34

Ian turned over and swam a few strokes toward the bank, then he swam back and began treading water. He said, "I haven't asked you how you're feeling lately."

"That fascinating topic."

"Well, are you any better?"

"Sometimes, but then I get tired again. Mostly I'm bored, I guess. I don't really know anyone on this island anymore, not since I went away to school. It's funny how in a couple of years you lose touch. I don't have any real friends here any longer."

"Nobody to do anything with," Ian said.

"That's right. If I wanted to go to the beach, for instance, I'd probably have to go with Amanda."

"Tell you what," he said, "if it's nice Saturday, let's go. You're well enough, aren't you?"

"I don't see why not. I could just lie there if I got tired." And then she turned her head to look at him there beside her, treading water, and smiled. "Would you really like to do that?" she said. "I could show you a little of the island on the way."

And that seemed to settle it. She watched him wading out of the pond, stopping to shake himself the way a dog would, scattering the air with bright drops of water, before he stooped to pick up his towel. Floating, she watched him start up the path. He was whistling a tune she didn't recognize, switching his towel through the grass. She thought he was surprisingly easy to talk to. She was sorry when the sound of the whistling died away.

5

Saturday morning. When Kate came downstairs, she found Frances Hilmer in the kitchen with Amanda. They were standing at the table making large, sloppy sandwiches of ham and mayonnaise.

"Put mayonnaise on one piece of bread. Put mustard on the other," Frances was saying. Was commanding.

Amanda looked at her meekly. "Not on both?"

Amanda and Frances were friends of sorts because Amanda valued anyone who was older, and Frances, so far as Kate could tell, liked anyone she could push around. She was possibly the only person alive who could push Amanda.

"Are the two of you having a picnic?" Kate asked.

"We're all having a picnic," said Frances. "Didn't you know that?"

Kate turned around and looked at her. There was something about Frances that she really couldn't stand. "No," she said. "I didn't."

"Ian asked us," Amanda said.

"What do you mean he asked you?"

"He did," said Amanda. "Me and Frances."

Slowly Frances ran her tongue down the blade of the mayonnaise knife. Then she put the knife back into the jar. "He did," she said. "Why shouldn't he?"

Ian's car roared and strained on the hills. Kate could smell exhaust through the open window. Amanda and Frances, in the rear seat with an air mattress and the picnic cooler between them, held their breaths audibly every time there was a climb; let them out just as noisily when they had passed the hill's crest.

Kate turned around and looked at them. Frances was kicking the seat in front of her, sucking a strand of her long, stringy hair. "Frances was the Light Princess in her fifth grade play," said Amanda, as if she had known that at that very minute Kate had been thinking how much Frances looked like a troll. Kate didn't answer.

"Which beach are we going to?" she said.

"Gull," said Amanda. "It has the best waves." And then the two of them sucked in their breaths again as the car began to climb the next rise.

From the top of the hill there was suddenly a view of the ocean, shades of blue extending along a beige scarf of sand, and at the horizon, melting seamlessly into the sky. Kate always saw this view as if she were seeing it for the first time. Ian slowed the car. "Look at that," he said, which pleased Kate. She hated it when anyone got poetic about that view, as if, by describing it, they were trying to establish ownership. A view like that was something to see and let alone.

"It's the best view on the island," she said. "Usually there are ten cars up here with people taking pictures."

"You could never really get it in a photograph," he said, which pleased her, too.

Amanda kicked impatiently in the back seat, and Ian let the car coast down the hill. After that the hills were smaller and finally there was a downhill stretch all the way to the dunes. Frances jumped out, and Amanda followed, dragging the air mattress. "You've got to cross the dunes," said Amanda, "and then, *Watch Out!* You're going to see the biggest waves of your life!" She glanced at Frances.

"Ian is from California, you know," Kate said. The two of them were beginning to get on her nerves.

"But he doesn't get to the ocean all that much," said Amanda, and took off over the dunes, dragging the air mattress, leaving the sand ridged like corduroy.

"Is that true?" Kate said. "Don't you go to the ocean much out there?"

"I used to. Years ago my brother and I went all the time. But I don't so much now. I'm too busy."

Kate nodded. The idea of a brother—of a whole family somewhere in California—gave him a dimension she hadn't thought about before.

"Older brother?" she said.

38

"Older, tougher, taller, and smarter," Ian said. "At least that's what he thinks. He's a physicist. He can't understand what I'm doing in the history of art."

"Sisters, too?"

"One. She's about your age."

"Seventeen?"

"I think she is. She must be, though I always think of her as little." He smiled. "It's funny. When I think of my brother, it's always as an adult, but when I think of her, I remember this tiny little wagon she used to have. She'd pull it to the top of the hill behind our house and then sit there yelling for me. She didn't have the nerve to ride it down."

"So what would you do? Go get her?"

"Oh, sure. I always did. All I had to do was walk along beside the wagon and she'd get down fine. She just needed to be encouraged."

They followed the track of the air mattress across the sand. By the time they had climbed to the top of the dunes, the girls were at the water's edge, having left the air mattress halfway down the beach. "Come on, Ian!" Amanda yelled. "It isn't very cold!"

Kate lay on her stomach in the sand and watched the three of them jumping in the waves, trying to work their way out beyond the point where the waves were breaking, so they could ride them in. They bounced like corks on the rise and fall of the water, the girls' heads appearing one by one, and then Ian's, and then the roar and crash and foam of the wave.

Kate dug her toes into the sand, feeling her way down to where it was damp and cool. Gulls screamed overhead. A couple with small children trudged past, the children staggering behind their parents, ankle-deep in the soft sand. Kate rested her chin on her arms and looked at the water.

After a while the three of them came dragging back up the beach, laughing and dripping. "We almost got killed," said Amanda. "Those were the biggest waves of my life!"

"That true?" Kate said.

"I've seen bigger," said Frances.

Amanda paused on her way to the picnic cooler and glanced sideways at Frances. "Well, me too," she said. "I have sometimes. I think I just forgot." And then she began unpacking the lunch.

They ate in silence, watching the waves break. When they had finished, Frances and Amanda went off to feed crusts to the gulls. Ian stretched out on his back and closed his eyes. "When I was their age," he said, "my brother and I used to play Lawrence of Arabia at the beach. Naturally my brother was Lawrence."

"Always?"

"I told you he was bigger and stronger. He was Lawrence, and I was everything else, including the camels."

"I would have made him take turns."

"I guess I should have, but I didn't really care. The point was to do whatever I had to so he would include me."

"Even being a camel? What did you do when you were a camel?"

"Oh, carried supplies. Sometimes I carried *him*."

"And you didn't mind? I can't believe it."

"Well, you know, he was my older brother, and I wanted him to like me."

"And you gave up being Lawrence just so he'd like you?"

"Oh, I gave up being Lawrence, and I gave up my tent and my basketball—all of them at one time or another. I really needed him to like me."

Kate squinted across the expanse of sand to where the waves were breaking.

"Did it work?" she asked. "Did he like you?" And then the sand began to blur, and her eyes were full of tears. Kate stood up. "I'm going in the water," she said. And, without looking back, she began to run down the beach.

She could hear Ian calling to her, but she didn't stop. She splashed through the foam at the water's edge and threw herself under a wave as it broke. She came up on the other side and swam out toward the calmer water, taking long, rapid strokes until she felt her body begin to warm. Then she turned and bobbed gently in the moving water. She couldn't tell whether the salt taste in her mouth was ocean or tears.

She told herself it was ocean. The sudden tears made her furious. She blamed it on the damn disease and dipped her face into the water, letting the cold salt scrub her cheeks.

When she looked back at the beach, she could see the girls far down along the shore and Ian standing at the water's edge. She joggled on the surface, suspended between the warmth of the air and the chill of the sea. She knew she should go back.

She began to paddle toward the shore, moving slowly at first and then more quickly as the momentum of the waves caught her and began to rush her toward the sand. She rose with the water, paddling hard now, and shot toward the beach, carried on the wave's strength. She staggered out of the water, stopped to wring her hair, and started up the beach to Ian. Her face was wet, but only with sea water.

"I know I shouldn't have done that," she said before he could. "But it didn't hurt me." And then she flopped down on the hot sand, breathless and tired, and lay there feeling the salt begin to prickle as her skin dried.

In the car on the way home, Frances and Amanda were quiet, and after a mile or two, they were asleep, heads resting against opposite doors. The air was warm rushing past the open window. Kate was sleepy, too.

"It was a nice afternoon," Ian said. Kate glanced at him. His hair was still damp, curling at the back of his neck. It was exactly the color of a wet clay pot.

Then she looked out at the road curving through the hills of the up-island moraine, between low scrub oaks, then suddenly through open fields drowned in late afternoon sunlight.

"They look like Monets, those fields," Ian said.

"The light, you mean."

"It's all light. Light defines everything." And then, "One

thing I'm going to do before I go home is see the Impressionists in the Boston museum."

"At the Fine Arts," Kate said. "My father used to take me there."

That had been many years ago. Winter Sundays when she was small and they had not yet moved to the island; years when her father was teaching in Boston, sandwiching painting between classes. She could remember the striped sweater she had liked to wear, and her father holding her coat as she trailed after him from painting to painting.

"He tried to explain to me about technique," she said. "I remember him explaining about the way they broke up color."

And in her mind's eye, she could still see his arm sweeping the paintings, pointing, telling her what he saw.

"That must have been exciting for you," said Ian.

"It was." It had been the most exciting thing she could remember. Like entering into a special club—herself and her father, painters, among all these other painters whose works hung on the walls.

"I remember one painting I especially liked. A field of poppies. Just dabs of red, you know?" And Ian nodded, as if he knew the picture she meant. "I used to look at it a lot. I used to think I saw a rabbit in that field, living in a burrow in the upper right hand corner."

Kate hesitated, remembering the field and the red spots that were poppies, and the rabbit she had been sure was hiding there. She remembered her father's arm, sweeping the field like a mowing machine. "After a while I stopped seeing the rabbit," she said. "I decided it was a dumb idea."

"Dumb why?"

"Well, because it wasn't there."

"Who says?"

"Oh, I don't know. I suppose my father."

She leaned back against the seat and watched the fields slide by. "Anyway that was such a long time ago," she said. "Back in the days when I was going to be a painter."

Ian began to whistle. It was the tune Kate had heard and not recognized before. "What is that?" she said.

"A James Taylor song from the seventies. We used to listen to it in high school."

The notes blew out the window and Kate imagined them drifting away behind the car, clustering along the roadside like leaves in autumn. "You got burned today," she said.

Ian touched his nose, the back of his neck, and smiled. Kate felt drowsy and light-headed in the rush of warm air along the car's side. She rested her head against the door and listened to Ian whistling.

Mrs. Hilmer was waiting for Frances. Amanda stood on the grass waving them goodbye, and then she told Kate that she wanted the first shower. Lacking Frances, she was entirely herself again. Kate didn't care. "Just leave some hot water."

Kate sat on the back steps, knowing that she should get out of the sun, but not moving. She was thinking of the poppy field in the Boston museum and how often she had tried painting pictures of the meadow later in imitation.

Hunkering down beside her father on the studio floor with her paints spread out around her, she had spent most of a summer painting spots of color, trying to break up the light in the way he'd explained. She supposed that nobody, looking at those pictures now, would recognize what she had been trying to do, but she remembered how hard she'd tried, wanting so much to please him.

6

The days slid together. In the meadow, the lilies opened and closed. The wild rose petals had scattered weeks before, leaving deep red, fringed hips behind.

Along the edge of the meadow, the garden was in full bloom—a deep border of delphinium and lupine, bells of campanula, mounds of daisies. There were pale pink roses, lemon yellow lilies, and three varieties of marigolds. It surprised Kate that one of the pleasures of the summer was standing in that deep border with her mother, working among flowers.

Sometimes in the evening after dinner, Ian brought out his guitar and strummed it on the porch. One day he bought a kite in town and they flew it in the meadow—a green and white Chinese dragon that mounted the air unsteadily as Ian played out string.

He taught Kate some of the songs he knew. Mostly they were country songs filled with loneliness and broken hearts. Kate loved them. Sitting on the porch, they sang about homesick prisoners, betrayals, drownings, and lonesome engine whistles wailing through the night. But mostly they sang about love—love gone wrong, remembered, mourned. The sadder the songs were, the better Kate liked them. "You're like my sister," Ian said. "There's nothing that makes her happier than a really mournful song." And Kate nodded, smiling. She felt like a cork bobbing on this sea of misery. She felt light as the kite wobbling uncertainly in the evening sky.

She had a sense of time suspended—a luxury of time disturbed only a little by the thought that she wasn't getting enough work done. She woke with that thought in the morning. She lay in the comfortable cocoon of sheets, making plans. In the afternoon she traced Chinese dragons in the margins of her book.

Now, when she took coffee and mail to the studio in the morning, she delivered Ian's mail as well. It was no trouble, she told him. She didn't mind. She liked going around to the little storeroom, after she'd delivered her father's thermos, and tucking Ian's letters inside the door.

Sometimes, if he wasn't too busy, she stayed to talk. He had offered to explain to her about his cataloging and he did, in bits and pieces. Gradually she came to understand what he did—a good deal more than listing, as he'd said. There were measurements to take, photographs to collect, dates and circumstances to record on the file cards that he

47

kept in metal boxes. She listened to what he had to say, and left reluctantly.

It was Ian who was making the summer possible, and she knew it. It was because of him that she was content to drift through the days. There was something in his gentleness that made her gentle. Even her father bothered her less.

And he was being awful—her father. The painting wasn't going well. Kate could see this. Delivering the coffee in the morning, she noticed that the picture on the easel remained essentially unchanged from day to day. The struggle seemed to be consuming him, but the problem, whatever it was, remained unresolved. The spider line still cut across the canvas, inconclusive, wrong.

He paced back and forth, from window to easel. He called Ian in for, so far as Kate could tell, nothing. To tell him stories. To talk about pictures he had painted years before. It seemed that instead of painting, he was remembering painting, and he wanted Ian to listen. But the picture didn't change.

Sometimes when she came into the studio he was working and seemed hardly to notice she was there. Other times he would begin to talk as though he were continuing a conversation aloud that he'd been having with himself.

"Do you remember when we came to this island, Kate?"

Why ask that? Kate shook her head, hurrying to leave his thermos and take Ian his mail. "I remember being in Boston, and I remember suddenly being here. I don't remember moving."

"You were too young, I suppose."

"I guess." Through the wall she could hear the sound of Ian's typing. He typed with one finger, and the hurried pecking sound made her smile, thinking of the one finger searching its way over the keys.

"I don't suppose you remember all the articles in the papers."

"What articles?"

"Oh, there were a number of interviews, some articles about my leaving Boston and coming here. Ian found some old newspapers in one of the files. I've been looking them over today."

"Oh." Kate was trying to listen to the typing.

"I had a million ideas when we came to this island. I had a storehouse of paintings in my head."

Kate nodded, hardly hearing, edging toward the door. It didn't really matter whether she listened or not. As usual he was talking to himself.

His mood lay over the household like a low cloud, and they all felt it. One evening, watching her mother carry a tray of coffee out to the lawn after dinner, Kate noticed what care she had taken to see that the screen door didn't slam behind her. They had all begun to move like shadows, Kate thought, trying not to disturb him.

Only Amanda seemed oblivious. Their mother eased the screen door closed, but Amanda laughed out loud, whirling around and around on the grass, making herself dizzy. Kate could remember doing that, whirling until she was too dizzy to stand up, and falling and laughing, and standing up to whirl again. Watching Amanda, she felt time collapse like a telescope, felt almost dizzy with the memory.

Amanda stopped whirling and came staggering toward them. Around her neck was the inevitable lanyard, together with a few loose lengths of bright plastic string. "When Ian comes out, I'm going to teach him to braid," she said. "I got him his favorite colors." Then she looked at their father. "Why don't you paint a picture of me with my lanyard on?" she said. And when he didn't answer her, "Why don't you paint a huge big picture of the meadow? Put all the bugs in?"

Kate's mother laughed, and Kate, pouring coffee, stopped and glanced at her father.

If he had heard Amanda, he gave no indication that he had. Preoccupied, remote, he sat. "A great big huge picture," Amanda insisted, tugging at the arm of his chair. "Full of bugs." She waited a minute, looking at him inquiringly. Then, when he still failed to notice, she climbed up onto his knees and flopped into his lap.

"You could put in ladybugs and the ants and the caterpillars," she said, making the words into a kind of chant. "You could put in grasshoppers and worms. You could put in flowers, all the different kinds. And skunks. And rabbits."

Her voice went on, listing everything she could think of. Kate sat on the grass, slowly stirring her coffee, and watched the two of them. She had never been able to tug at his arm that way, to plop without ceremony into his lap. That was Amanda, easy, casual, unaware. But it had never been Kate.

As she watched, Amanda reached up and hugged him around the neck. "Talk to me, big old Father," she said. And finally he looked at her and patted her head, mussing her hair with a hand still paint-stained.

The next morning Leah's letter arrived. Kate found it among the rest of the mail, a violet envelope lying amid the usual scatter of advertisements and bills. Walking up the driveway from the mailbox, she ripped open the flap. Leah wanted to come for the weekend. Long Island was dull.

Kate carried the letter, together with the rest of the mail, around to the back of the house where her mother was staking delphinium. "Leah wants to come for the weekend," she said.

Her mother straightened up, standing waist-high among blue and deep blue and purple flowers. She frowned. "Which weekend?"

"This one. She's bored."

Her mother hesitated, looking toward the studio before turning back. She was wondering, Kate knew, whether this would disturb him. Every decision her mother made now was filtered through this concern, as though, by protecting him, she could somehow single-handedly make his painting go right again. Frowning, she moved a stake from hand to hand. Then she seemed to turn a corner. "Why not?" she said. "Tell her to come."

Kate dropped off her father's mail, then Ian's. "My roommate's coming for the weekend," she said. "You'll like her. Everyone does." Ian nodded, distracted. It seemed that the mood of the house lay heavy on him, too.

"I'm trying to think of what we'll do while she's here," Kate said. But she could see that Ian didn't want to talk, so she left his mail and closed the door.

All week, off and on, she wondered what Leah would want to do. If Long Island bored her, what, Kate wondered, would she think of this place where so little happened from day to day, and where, now, they all moved silent as ghosts, trying not to disturb her father. She wondered, but it was no use worrying because Leah was coming and that was that.

And then it was Friday and Leah was there.

There she was, sitting in the middle of Kate's bed in her nightgown, saying, "But he's just marvelous, Kate! He's darling! Why didn't you ever tell me your father was like that?" And Kate, brushing her hair with her back to Leah, was thinking, Why wouldn't she think he was wonderful? He had transformed himself.

All evening he had been charming, funny, almost poetic, as if nothing at all were on his mind but the pleasure of the moment. He had taken them to town for ice cream. Ice cream! This man who never went to town.

Who would have known that his mood had lain on the house like a yellow fog for weeks? It had lifted like a curtain going up, and on such a scene, such a performance!

"He's magic, Kate. He's unreal."

Kate twisted her hair into a knot and clipped it. "He's real," she said.

7

It had begun at dinner. Or maybe before that. Leah blew in—her plane a half hour late—like a long-awaited change in the weather. She liked everything about the island at once, and everyone liked her. Before they had gotten her suitcase across the kitchen and up the stairs, she had made fast friends of Kate's mother and Amanda.

Kate had seen this happen before. In classes she had watched one teacher after another start to smile when Leah started talking. There was something about her that no one could resist. And at dinner it was the classroom all over again. Leah talked and everyone was smiling.

"This place is enchanted," Leah said. "I knew it would be. Nothing at all like Long Island."

Amanda rested the bowl of her spoon on her lip and stared.

"That place is one long boutique," Leah said. "I don't have anything against boutiques, but who needs the stuff most of those places sell? That's what amazes me. People come in and buy soap that looks like crayons. Five dollars. Patchwork cocktail napkins. Handmade. Who cares if they're handmade?"

She shook her head, and Kate's mother laughed. "What else?"

"Oh, you know, everything useless." And then she paused. "But I bet you *don't* know. This place is so different."

"We have our share of that kind of thing. You haven't been to town yet."

Leah looked unconvinced. "Down there all you see is a lot of people walking around with designer labels on their rears. But this place is perfect."

And then she turned to Kate's father.

"I brag about you all the time," she said. "I tell people that I room with Marcus Brewer's daughter and they say 'Wow' or something like that. I mean, they're impressed. When I told my parents I was actually going to meet you, they were dazzled."

Kate's father bowed his head and smiled.

"Haven't you ever met our dad?" Amanda said.

Leah shook her head. "How could she have?" said Kate. "He hasn't come to school for two years. Not since I roomed with Leah."

"But now I have," said Leah. "And it's all true what the articles say. I looked up some articles in the library. And, of course, I saw the TV segment."

54

"You're very thoughtful," Kate's father said. "And you're swelling my head to a terrible size."

Kate looked across the table at Leah. There wasn't a feature of her narrow little face or wiry little body that you could single out to admire. Her eyes were small and too close together. She was very thin. But she was lovely all the same—a fresh breeze making everyone smile.

Kate's mother offered second helpings. Ian reached for Leah's plate.

"This sole may be the best sole I have ever eaten," Leah said. "It's unreal."

"I think that you're a believer in magic," Kate's father said, and Leah laughed as though she had never heard anything quite so amusing before.

It was a long dinner. By the time they had finished, the sun had set and they drank coffee in twilight, still sitting around the table.

"What would you think," Kate's father said suddenly, "of driving into town for ice cream?"

Kate glanced at him, startled. He went to town perhaps once a summer, if he went that often.

"Think of the crowds in town," her mother said. "You know what the weekends are like."

But he was firm, and at the same time lighthearted, as though he had planned a special entertainment for them and wouldn't be denied. He raised his arms, conducting them like an orchestra, and they rose from the table and piled into the station wagon in the barn.

The town was just as Kate's mother had said it would

be. The sidewalks were full of after-dinner strollers. There was a line outside the movie theater, a line to buy ice cream at the outdoor stand near the harbor. Children on bicycles shared the street with a steady stream of cars. The last ferry, preparing to leave, honked a short, mournful warning, and the passengers still lingering on the dock began to move.

"You see, Marcus, it'll take an hour to get near the ice cream stand," Kate's mother said. He seemed not to hear her.

He led them past the jostling crowd waiting at the lighted stand, along the street that fronted on the harbor, to an outdoor cafe with umbrella-shaded tables. And here he stopped and smiled as though he had conjured up the cafe with the wave of a wand.

He insisted that they push two tables together to accommodate them all, and a waiter appeared out of nowhere. A college student, Kate guessed, but with all the gestures of a continental waiter. He recognized her father. "You see?" Leah said, "You see what I mean? Everybody knows you."

Kate's father insisted on ordering for them and, again, it seemed to Kate that Italian ices appeared out of nowhere, rushed to the table in a rainbow of colors. "This is more than we can possibly eat," Kate's mother said, but her father waved away the comment.

There was a sliver of moon above the harbor, and the sound of a piano coming from someplace further down the wharf. People passed, ambling along, and glanced in at the tables and their yellow-striped umbrellas. A long-haired cat wove its way between the chairs, soft and gray as smoke. The ferry began to pull out, slipping silently away through the mirroring harbor, spangling the water with lights.

"I *know* you would like it," Kate's father was saying. "You must make it a point to go there sometime."

Kate turned away from the lights on the water. "Go where?" she asked.

"Venice," said Leah. "Your father lived there once."

Kate nodded, because, of course, she knew.

"It's a place," said her father, "that, once you've seen, you'll never forget."

"*This* is a place I'll never forget," said Leah. She leaned back in her chair and smiled at Kate. "You know what it makes me think of?" she said. "It's the way I imagine Prospero's island. Kind of dreamy, you know?"

"But," said Kate's father, "you haven't seen Venice." He leaned forward, stroking the air. "There are evenings when the city seems to float," he said, "seems made of clouds. There are days when you would swear that the sunlight had been spun out of spider web and that the buildings had been spun out of sugar."

Leah leaned forward slowly, moving as if she were mesmerized. She rested on her elbows, sucking her spoon.

"The light there is like no other light on earth," he said. "The canals are like green ribbon. Of all the cities in the world, it is the most romantic, the most like a city of fairy tales. It's exactly the place for someone who believes in magic.

"Early in the morning, there are wisps of mist on the canals, white mist that rises and disperses in the sunlight, leaving nothing but its memory, the way dreams do."

It seemed to Kate that his voice contained dreams. She shifted uncomfortably, glanced from face to face. Her mother leaned over to mop a dribble on Amanda's shirt. Across the table, Ian smiled.

"Venice is a place to go when you're young," her father said.

And Leah nodded, coming to. "I wish you'd tell my father that," she said. "His idea of romantic is Pittsburgh."

"Pittsburgh has its points," said Kate's mother. "I was born there."

"Does it?" Leah looked at her absently. "But Venice, though—"

"Venice is as far from Pittsburgh as we are from the moon," Kate's father said, and nodded at the sliver of moon overhead, as though he had produced that, too, especially for their pleasure.

Kate looked from him to Leah. And then at the melting ices, and finally at the moon curled in the sky. And none of it seemed real. A scrim of sky to which a delicate curve of moon was pinned, silver dishes full of rainbows, a cat, a chorus of strolling couples, and music that seemed to come out of the air. Kate had a curious feeling that the rest of them were onlookers, observing some scene spun out by an enchanter.

On the way home Amanda fell asleep. Kate's mother

cradled her head. Leah began to sing in a voice as thin and clear as the moonlight. One by one they all joined in, until, by the time they had reached the barn, even Kate's father was singing.

And now Leah sat in the middle of Kate's bed, waiting while Kate finished brushing her hair. Leah was staring at the ceiling. "He's wonderful," she said. "All that about Venice. He had me hypnotized."

"I've never heard him talk that way before," Kate said. "I've heard him talk about Venice often enough, but not in that way. Usually he talks about how some painter did light or water."

"I suppose he thought I wouldn't understand about painting light and water," said Leah. "Which I wouldn't."

Kate nodded, pulled off her shirt, and dropped her nightgown over her head. Then she walked across the room to turn out the light.

But she couldn't sleep. Long after she knew that Leah was asleep—could hear the slow rhythm of her breathing—she lay awake watching a cloud like a puff of smoke in the sky.

At last she got up and went to stand beside the window looking down over the meadow. There was still a light in the storeroom, spreading fanwise onto the grass. She supposed Ian was reading or maybe even working late. She leaned against the window frame, looking at the night.

She had stood this way before, many dozen times as a child, slowly sinking to her knees, resting her chin on the windowsill, almost too sleepy to keep watch over the lights that blossomed magically in the studio below, where her father was painting. Sometimes she had fallen asleep on the floor, but often she had seen the lights go out one by one, had hurried into bed, and had waited to hear his step on the stair, hoping that he would remember to come into her room to kiss her goodnight.

8

*After breakfast Kate found Leah in the sitting room, look-*ing at snapshots with Mrs. Hilmer. They were slowly going through the plastic pockets in Mrs. Hilmer's worn billfold, pausing over each one. The pictures, of course, were of Frances.

Kate had seen some of them. Frances, age three, in her Easter bonnet. Frances on her first day of school. She supposed there were plenty of others by now that she hadn't seen.

"What I'd like is a nice oil portrait like the one up there," Mrs. Hilmer was saying as Kate came into the room. She shrugged. "Anyway," she said, "there she is on Hallow-een."

Leah made a sympathetic, clucking sound. "A pirate," she said.

"That's right. Nothing would do but she'd be a pirate."
Mrs. Hilmer laughed affectionately. "That girl has a mind
of her own."

Kate glanced at the snapshot in the cloudy plastic pocket.
Frances—a troll in a pirate suit.

"It's kind of nice the way she carries all those pictures
around," Leah said later, and Kate could see that she really
thought it was nice.

"What she wants is for my father to paint a portrait,"
Kate said. "Which is never going to happen."

"Why don't you, then?" Leah said.

"Why don't I? You're crazy."

"You know how to paint. I can remember freshman
year everyone was talking about how Marcus Brewer's
daughter was in school and how she was an artist. Long
time before I met you, I knew that. And then I remember
you won a prize in that exhibit. I never could see why you
switched to English."

" 'I know my mind and I have made my choice; Not
from your temper does my doom depend—' "

"What are you talking about?"

"That's Edna St. Vincent Millay," Kate said. "Overall,
a fairly sappy poet."

They were sitting on the porch steps in the sun, sharing
a bunch of grapes.

"I guess I'm going to be looking at pictures all morning,"
Leah said. "Your father said I could come down to the
studio if I wanted, and naturally I do."

"When?" said Kate.

62

"Whenever. Want to go now?"

"You're the one he invited."

"Well, naturally he meant you, too, stupid." And Leah plucked a grape and tipped back her head and opened her mouth and dropped it in.

He pulled out paintings one by one, propping them around the walls of the studio as though the room were a gallery. Of course Kate had seen them all, knew the kinds of things he would say, and so she followed along for a little while, and then wandered off toward the windows.

The studio was hot. Sun came slanting through the skylights. The ladder-back chair where she'd sat to pose was still there, against the wall. It was funny, she thought, how chairs and light and pictures remained the same year to year, that it was only the people who altered.

It might have been herself instead of Leah who trailed after him around the room. The room might have been one of the galleries in the Boston museum. Kate remembered how she had had to hurry to keep up with him, clutching at his tweed jacket to try to slow him down since he would never have thought to slow otherwise.

And now she was so long-legged that she could keep up with anyone. She was too long-legged to curl her toes comfortably around the rungs of the chair the way she once had done, feeling the smooth painted wood on her bare feet and the sun on her knees, watching her father move forward and back from the easel, engaged in his rapt slow dance with the canvas. That summer when, humming tunelessly, he would glance at her, seeming, she thought, to invite her to join in the dancing.

It was so hot that they swam off and on all afternoon. Heat hung over the meadow thick as wool, almost solid.

When they were not in the water, they lay in the sun on the grassy bank and talked about friends at school, about classes. And then, too hot to talk, they went back into the water. Leah wore her fuchsia bikini. Kate thought it had been a good choice. The color suited her. She looked like a flamingo, standing balanced on one foot at the edge of the pond.

"So are you getting your work made up?" she asked.

"Not as fast as I thought I would. The paper is taking forever."

"Still having trouble with Prospero?"

Kate nodded. "I just can't like him."

"You don't have to like him to write about him, do you?"

"No. But I come on lines that infuriate me, and then I lose my concentration. All that stuff about what a terrific father he's been, for instance."

"You still don't think he's good to Miranda?"

Kate said nothing for a minute, and then she said, "You know what I think."

She put her head on her arms and looked at the blades of grass growing inches from her nose, so close that the minute shadings of green along their lengths were discernible.

Leah came back and sat down on her towel. She began smearing suntan oil on her arms. "I was thinking when we were in the studio this morning how much time I used to spend there," Kate said. "Not just posing. I used to paint there. My father bought me paints—much better paints than the kind you'd ordinarily buy for a child. I'd take them down there and paint beside him." Kate laughed. "I had this idea he was teaching me to be just like him."

Leah hunched and looked at her shoulder, checking it for burn. "Well, he was, wasn't he? He was teaching you to paint."

Kate shrugged. "Who knows what he was doing? Anyway, it ended. I came home from school for Christmas, freshman year, and he told me that I'd probably better start painting someplace besides the studio."

"Why?"

"He said it was too crowded."

Kate sat up and hugged her knees. "But I think that was just an excuse. I don't think he liked me being there. I'd gotten too serious about painting. It was all right so long as I was just a little girl messing around with watercolors, but freshman year I won that prize. They hung that exhibit for Parents' Weekend, remember?"

"In October. Sure."

Kate nodded. "My parents were coming for the weekend. I'd kept the prize a secret, mostly, I think, because I wanted to see my father's face when he discovered I'd won it. I thought he'd be so pleased."

She pulled blades of grass from between her toes, and

65

twisted them, making a tiny crushed green rope between her fingers. "I counted down the days to the weekend," she said. Then she smiled. "I got my ears pierced."

"You what?"

"Got my ears pierced. I went into town and got them done."

"What's that got to do with anything?"

"I don't know. It's just part of what I remember about that week." She remembered, too, the blouse she'd borrowed. And the brand-new gold studs in her ears. She could still see the trees spreading fire colors along the hills behind the school, and feel the flutter of excitement that last day, waiting, dressing, getting ready.

"Anyway," she said, "they finally got there. My father walked into the exhibit, and at first there was all the usual hullabaloo—everyone wanting to meet him. And he was charming. My father, as you've seen, can be very charming when he feels like it. He said all the right things. You know, every inch the artist."

"And?"

"And finally we got to my picture. There it was with its first-prize ribbon."

"And?"

"Well, he looked. And I looked at him." Kate shrugged.

How could she describe his expression? It had been so odd. Even now she could think of no words to describe it. "Then," she said, "some woman came up to him and began saying all this stuff about wasn't it wonderful to have two such terrific painters in the family. You know the kind of ridiculous things people say, just talking? Two Brewers now—that kind of thing. And my father—," Kate stopped. "And my father smiled at her and said, 'It's a nice little picture.' A nice little picture! As if it was some crayon drawing of Amanda's! As if he couldn't tell the difference! Then he started telling her about some show of his that was opening in New York."

"But, of course, he could tell the difference, Kate."

"I know. That's the worst part."

Leah looked confused. Kate couldn't blame her. She had been confused herself for months after that.

"Fathers get funny," Leah said.

"You don't have to say that."

"They do, though. Sometimes mine treats me like I was an electric fence."

Kate had to smile at this idea, and to smile, too, at Leah's efforts to make things somehow better. Then she took a deep breath. "Anyway," she said, "after that I stopped painting. Not right away. When I went back to school after Christmas, I was going to paint all the time. I was going to learn everything there was to know without him." She laughed. "I planned to get so good that when someone mentioned 'Brewer' they'd mean me, Kate. But after a while I couldn't even go near the art room. The smell of the paints made me sick."

Leah didn't say anything. She rocked herself gently back and forth, staring at her feet.

"Why didn't you ever tell me any of this before?" she said finally.

"What for? What difference would it make? It's ancient history. I suppose the only reason I'm telling you now is that being home all summer keeps reminding me. Last night reminded me. You know, Leah, my father has never treated me the way he treated you last night."

"You're his daughter, for God's sake!"

"What's that got to do with it?"

"I'm telling you, Kate, that's the way they are. They get funny. I think we make them nervous."

"No," Kate said, "that's not it."

She sat looking out across the pond, at the agitation of dragonflies above the lily pads. When she looked back, Leah was bent over examining her toes.

"What it is, Leah, is this," she said. "My father has to have the foreground all to himself. He has to be the center of attention. It took me longer than it should have to understand that. I thought that the way to please him was to become a better and better painter. After that business at school, I saw that I was wrong."

"So you stopped trying to please him."

Kate shook her head slowly. "I stopped painting."

After dinner they swam again and then they lay in the grass beside the house and watched heat lightning flickering in the sky until nearly midnight. Ian sat with them for a while. Amanda sat. One by one, everyone came out and sat for a little and watched the lightning fret at the sky before they wandered off to bed.

"It's like scribbles up there," Leah said.

"That's funny," Kate said. "I've always thought the same thing. Someone enormous up there painting with incandescent paint."

Leah stretched. "I'm getting sleepy."

There were no lights in the studio now, not many in the house.

"You like Ian a lot, don't you?" said Leah.

"What makes you say so?"

"Observation."

"He's really made all the difference this summer," Kate said.

On Sunday morning it began to rain, and it was still raining in the afternoon when Leah began packing. "I hate to leave," she said.

Kate, sitting on the bed, watched the suitcase begin to fill. "Stay then."

"I can't. I have to go back and earn the money I've spent." Leah kept cramming things into the corners of her bag, but Kate could tell from the expression on her face that she had something else on her mind. Finally she said, "Okay, Leah. What are you thinking about?"

Leah glanced up from the suitcase, looking half-guilty. "Oh, I was just thinking about what you said yesterday. That seems like a kind of dumb reason not to paint."

"I agree. Very dumb."

"So why not paint then?"

"Oh," Kate shook her head. It wasn't anything she could explain. It was just something she couldn't do, though she knew it made no difference at all.

They drove to the airport in the rain, windshield wipers clicking.

"You know you can come down to visit any time you want," Leah said.

"What would I do while you're working?"

Leah hesitated, laughed. "Shop for handmade cocktail napkins," she said.

At the airport there was barely time to check Leah's bag before she was running for the plane. She was always late. She always would be. And that, for some reason, Kate thought, was a part of why she liked Leah.

Kate stood against the fence and watched the absurdly small plane begin to taxi across the field. She watched it lift, frail as a butterfly, into the clouds, then vanish on its way to Boston.

CHAPTER

9

Each time she drove into town now, Kate found the streets more crowded. The summer people were arriving in great numbers. Daily the ferries disgorged them—day-trippers with backpacks and bicycles who headed for the closest beaches; day-trippers who wandered through the shops along the harbor, buying souvenirs; whole families coming for a longer stay, arriving in station wagons so loaded down that the frames dragged coming off the boats. Dogs on leashes, tents, snorkels and flippers—every conceivable thing came off on the dock when the ferries pulled in toward the end of June.

The local paper called these summer days a carnival, but Kate didn't agree. Like any island native, she avoided the streets near the harbor in the summertime, and took vastly circuitous routes going in and out of town. Most of the trips she made were for her checkups or to take Amanda to meet the camp bus.

The purpose of the checkups was vague. The doctor told her each time to be patient and sooner or later the disease would go away. The nurse drew blood, taped a wad of cotton in the crook of Kate's arm covering the needle's small mosquito hole, and then Kate went home. Today had been no different.

She drove with one hand, resting the other on the open window ledge. The road, once it curved out of town, was empty, unrolling ahead of the car like a hot black ribbon. Kate leaned back in the seat, snapped on the radio, and followed the melting yellow center line.

She was thinking about Ian. He would like to hear about the woman in the doctor's waiting room who had swallowed a needle because she hadn't known it was there. He would laugh. "How could she have not known?" he would say, which was exactly the question Kate had wanted to ask herself.

She would tell him about the fat baby playing on the office floor, making a maze of plastic beads through which all the patients had had to pick their way. She saw Ian quite often now at the pond in the afternoon, and she thought she was beginning to know what he thought was funny.

She turned right and started up the last hill home. The fields on either side of the road were as empty and still as the town had been bustling. At the top of the ridge, the house came into view. From this height, the house, the meadow, and the studio floating in the meadow were like a picturebook landscape. At school, when she thought about the island, it was this view she imagined, this tiny landscape reduced to toy size, viewed with a sea gull's detachment.

She could see a car in the driveway, sun glinting off its windshield, and then a figure coming around the side of the house. She let off the brake and coasted down the hill. When she turned into the driveway, she saw Ian sitting on the porch step. He was hammering.

Kate climbed out of the car and slammed the door. She kicked off her sandals and walked across the grass. "What are you doing?"

Ian looked up at her and grinned. "Hammering."

"Well, I mean—"

"You've got a loose board in the step."

"We've always had a loose board in the step."

"I'm fixing it."

Kate sat down on the top step to watch. "You know what I saw at the doctor's?" she said. "There was a woman there who'd swallowed a needle."

"What for?"

Kate laughed. "She swallowed it because she didn't know it was there."

"How could she not—," Ian began, and Kate laughed harder.

"I knew you'd say that. That's what I wanted to ask her, but I didn't have the nerve."

Ian was holding three nails in his teeth and managing to talk around them. That made Kate laugh, too. A breeze ruffled the leaves of the hydrangea beside the porch. It was a lovely day. "Who's here?" Kate said, nodding toward the unfamiliar car in the driveway.

"A professor from Baltimore to see your father."

"Is he getting the ordinary or the royal treatment?"

Ian looked blank.

"I mean is Mother showing him around or has my father turned up?"

"He's been out in the studio most of the morning talking with your father."

"Oh," said Kate, "then he must be a *very* important professor."

Ian took the nails out of his mouth and laid them one by one on the step.

"I mean," Kate said, "my father doesn't see many people."

"If your father saw all the people who want to see him about something or other, he'd never find time to paint."

"I know that," Kate said. "Believe me, I've heard that all my life. Other kids got lullabies. I got this tune about don't bother Daddy, he's a great painter."

She stopped. She had meant to make him laugh, but she could see that he wasn't going to.

"Your father *is* a great painter," Ian said. "That's the thing. And if you're as great a painter as your father, all kinds of people want things from you. He's right not to let them eat him up."

Kate looked at him thoughtfully. He sounded like her mother. She had heard this said all her life one way or

74

another. "Well, then, maybe great painters shouldn't have families," she said, saying the words before she knew they were there.

Ian looked up, and then went back to positioning a nail. Kate watched him lift the hammer. She shouldn't have said that. She hadn't known she was going to. It was like asking him to take sides. And, of course, that was wrong. He couldn't take sides. He hadn't come to the island to be her friend. He was here to do her father's cataloging.

Kate bent forward to pick up her sandals. She felt awkward. She had spoiled things. And now there seemed nothing else to say. The words were out and hanging in the air between them. She felt as if she had a needle stuck in her throat.

The professor stayed to dinner, and afterward there were a lot of dishes. Somehow Amanda had enticed Frances Hilmer to spend the night. "Since I have a guest," she said, "I shouldn't have to help."

"That's what you think," Kate said. "You can both help." She was in no mood to be nice to Amanda and Frances.

"I don't think that's fair," Amanda said. "All winter I have to help while you're at school."

"Tough," Kate said.

"If you clear, I'll start washing." Ian was standing in the kitchen doorway, and Kate supposed he had heard the whole thing.

"No," she said. "Amanda can do it. It's her job."

"I really don't mind."

"He really doesn't *mind,* Kate. So why don't you just let him? It might even be fun doing dishes with *Ian.*" This last Amanda said in a singsong voice, grinning evilly at Frances.

"All right," Kate said. "Get out of here."

"First I have to get my bug jar."

"Oh no you don't. Either you're gone in one second or you do them all."

She watched the two of them go out the door, looking back, giggling.

"You're spoiling her," Kate said to Ian, "and she's spoiled enough already." Then she pulled open the dishwasher door. "You don't have to help," she said. "I can do them."

But he was already scraping plates, so she shrugged and began piling dishes onto the drainboard.

"This makes me feel at home," Ian said. "My sister and I do dishes all the time."

"But not your brother?"

"Oh, hell no. He's too strong and tall and intelligent." And Kate laughed.

He hummed as he worked, scraping and rinsing. Kate stacked up the last of the dishes from the table, and started to load the dishwasher's rubberized slots.

The room was still warm with the afternoon's heat. In the heavy blue pitcher on the window ledge, her mother's lilies had begun to close, dribbling pollen on the sill. A fly crawled lazily along the edge of the sink. Kate worked mechanically, easing plates one by one into the machine.

They worked without talking. Kate could hear the rattle of coffee cups on the back lawn, the sound of the little girls' voices. Ian hummed softly, scraping and rinsing. In the cluster of sounds there was quiet.

He handed her a plate dripping water. He handed her a bouquet of forks. They worked together in a slow, easy rhythm, as if they had worked together for years.

The voices drifted in from the lawn. Kate heard her mother laughing. "You're nice to help," she said to Ian. And then, "You'd probably rather be out there with the rest of them."

Ian handed Kate a wine glass. "Nope," he said, and began rinsing spoons.

Kate waited, expecting to hear the polite next words that would make his "no" a courteous lie. But he said nothing else. He handed her the spoons, and Kate smiled.

Last they did pots. Ian propped them to dry on the drainboard. Kate mopped the kitchen table with a towel. Then she asked if he wanted coffee. "There's still a little left in the pot."

"Don't you want some?"

Kate shook her head. "I thought I might walk down to the salt marsh," she said. She paused, folding the checkered dish towel over her arm. Hesitating, she said, "Come with me if you want to."

10

They set off across the neighboring meadow through newly mown stubble, still green and fragrant. The remnants of an old stone boundary wall, tumbledown but never cleared away, snaked erratically along the field's edge.

They startled a flicker into flight. It swooped suddenly out of a thicket of wild roses, scolding and flapping above them. Kate looked up at its agitated wings. "There must be a nest around here," she said.

"Isn't it pretty late for nests?"

"Yes, but that's how they act if you're near one."

"Mothers are all the same," Ian said, "Birds or people— no difference."

Kate laughed, watching the flapping, scolding bird. High above a gull soared, strong and oblivious, slicing a powerful arc in the sky.

At the end of the field, they stopped and looked back. Kate could see Amanda at the edge of the meadow. Ahead of them was a sand track that ran aimlessly along the edge of the salt marsh. "It might go nowhere," Kate said, "or it might go all the way to the lighthouse. See?" she said. "You can just see the lighthouse there beyond the ridge."

"Is it too far to walk?" Ian said.

"Too far to get there and back before dark."

"Too far for you, I meant."

"I don't think so. If it is, we can turn back."

The track ran along for a ways and then it ran out, and they walked overland again through fields where the evening sounds of insects had begun in the grass. They walked side by side, not talking much. The sun dropped slowly toward the horizon, leaving yellow and apricot stains in the sky. Birds skimmed overhead—smooth, dark shapes in the yellow light. Kate began to smell the sea. She wondered whether Ian could smell it, but she didn't ask. The quiet was something they were sharing between them, a cone of lemon and apricot light.

After a while they found another sand road—two tracks separated by grass—that climbed gradually uphill toward the cliffs where the lighthouse stood. "Not too tired?" Ian asked, and Kate shook her head. One in each track, they started to climb with the grade, the daylight draining down the sky around them.

Kate could begin to hear the sound of the ocean breaking against the base of the cliffs. Gulls swooped over the cliff tops, dropping down again out of sight. All at once the beacon flashed, throbbing like a pulse. "Oh look," Kate said, and they stopped and waited until the light had swung out toward the sea.

"Can you run?" Ian said. "Let's see if we can get to the top before it swings around again." And they began to run, stumbling in the rutted tracks. All at once it was too dark to see. Kate ran, faltering after Ian, tripping over roots and stones, over her own feet in her effort to keep up.

At the top she was breathless, entirely worn out. "But look," she said, "we made it." And the beacon swung over them again.

Kate sank down on a rock and leaned back. The lighthouse was still above them, on a rise, behind a Coast Guard fence. "Climb on up if you want to," she said. "I think I have to sit."

He climbed a little way and she watched him. His shirt reminded her of a white moth moving in the darkness, until suddenly, momentarily, it was lit by the throb of the beacon. "Hear the ocean?" she called.

But of course he heard it. It rumbled like thunder against the cliffs. "If it were daylight, we could climb down," she called.

She didn't know whether he could still hear her—she could only just make out the flicker of his shirt—and then the beacon flashed and she could see that he had turned and was coming back.

He ran down the last bit of hill, sending a scatter of pebbles sliding ahead. He came around the rock and sat down beside her. "From up there, you can see the waves beginning to break when the light flashes that way," he said.

"Every time the water runs out, it's dyed with clay," Kate said. "They're made of red clay, the cliffs are."

Looking at him, she could just see the pale outlines of his face in the darkness. "When we were children, we used to paint the rocks along the shore with handfuls of red clay. It was like finger painting, only on an enormous scale. Afterwards we washed off in the sea. We called it 'painting the ocean.' All around us the water turned red.

"I always wanted to paint an entire rock," she said, "but they're huge and I wasn't big enough. I used to wish I were a sea gull so that I could reach the top."

He didn't answer, and suddenly Kate was afraid that she had bored him with her talk of painting rocks and sea gulls. "Well, anyway," she said. "It was just something we used to like to do."

She looked up at him. The beacon flashed again, and she saw, in the brief sweep of light across his face, that he was looking at her, and that he had been listening as if he cared about what she had to say.

"You really *do* love painting, don't you?" he said.

And Kate shrugged a little shrug. "Well, rocks."

"We walked all the way to the lighthouse," she said.

Her mother stopped weeding and sat back on her heels. "I wondered where you'd gone. We looked around for you after dark. It never crossed my mind you'd walk all that way."

"It didn't bother me at all," Kate said. "I felt fine."

Her mother looked at her thoughtfully, balancing her trowel on her knee. "That's a long walk," she said.

"I told you I felt fine. It didn't hurt me."

"No. Well."

Kate was too familiar with her mother's ways to think that this was all she had on her mind. She watched her scratching between tomato plants and waited to hear what else she would say. Their conversations often took this path, sidling crablike through a series of indirections toward the point.

"Ian is a nice person," her mother said.

"Are you just noticing that?"

"Of course, he's twenty-five."

"Which isn't exactly antique."

"It's eight years older than you are."

Kate looked at her mother inquiringly. "Okay," she said, "what is it that you're trying to say?"

Her mother's face was dim in the shade of her straw hat, embellished with a stroke of mud, and slightly embarrassed. Damp wisps of hair, escaping the hat's crown, clung to her forehead. "Are you possibly trying to say that Ian's too old for me? Are you worried because we went for a walk?"

"Not worried."

Kate laughed, oddly pleased. "Don't be silly," she said. "We're just friends."

And that was true, she thought. He was here to do a job for her father, but he was also her friend.

82

Her mother went back to weeding and Kate knelt beside her. She could feel the damp earth through the knees of her jeans. The tomato plants were filled with blossoms, yellow stars among the ragged green foliage. Later acid green bubbles would appear to replace the flowers, and, later still, there would be the avalanche of ripe fruit, filling bushel baskets, lined up in rows on the windowsills in the kitchen. But that would all be later. A month from now. She tugged at a weed contentedly, and inched her way down the row of plants behind her mother.

"Amanda will certainly miss him when he's gone," her mother said.

"He hasn't said anything about going."

"No, but he will, you know. He has his life in California."

"I do know that," Kate said, and then she laughed, remembering the flicker. "Stop acting like a mother bird," she said.

All afternoon Kate lay flat on her stomach beside the pond reading Shakespeare. She lay reading with her head in her hands, then with her head on her arms, and finally with her chin on the edge of the book. In that position she couldn't see much, but it didn't matter. For half an hour, she hadn't known what she was reading. Her mind kept slipping away from the lines on the page. It was like the lighthouse beacon, pausing on one thought and then on another, but not lingering.

She wondered whether Shakespeare had ever lived on a real island, or had only imagined one. She wondered what he meant Prospero to represent. In class, some people had said he was meant to represent the artist, creating illusion from reality. Others had said, no, the whole play was meant to be political. And then, of course, there was Leah's version—the sweet, white-haired old magician, and who cared what else he might represent.

Well, Kate thought, she *had* to care if she was going to write the paper, but she felt so drowsy, so content to lie sleepily in the sun.

She got up and walked down to the water. She sat on the bank and buried her feet in the soft silt of the pond's bottom. She thought about the bird's nest still containing eggs and about the tomato plants still in flower. Ian had said that he had quite a lot of work left to do. Thinking these things made space and time around her, the way saying "only June" had when she was a child hoarding summer.

11

Saturday morning Kate almost fell over Frances Hilmer in the downstairs hall. Frances was sitting on the floor with a coloring book and one of those boxes of crayons that contains every imaginable color, even gold and silver.

"Look out," she said when Kate stepped around her.

"*You* look out."

Frances was coloring a picture of Princess Di, being careful to stay within the lines.

"Other people have to walk through here," Kate said. "Why don't you pick up your crayons?"

Frances looked at her with eyes as cool and blue as a Siberian husky's. She said nothing, but scooped the strewn crayons into a pile.

There was mail on the hall table, stacked as Mrs. Hilmer stacked it—like a regiment prepared for drill. Kate shuffled through it and found a letter from Leah. A pink envelope this time, and inside, pink paper. A thank-you note.

"Did you get a letter?" Frances asked.

"Looks that way."

"Who from?"

Kate stopped reading and glanced at Frances. "From a friend of mine. Does it matter?"

Frances went back to working on Princess Di.

"What did your friend say?"

Kate started to tell her, then stopped. "None of your business, Frances," she said. She knew that Leah would have said something nice, but she couldn't. She felt surrounded by Frances.

"You know, Frances," she said—a stab at being nicer—"you could get some blank paper and make pictures of your own. That's better than coloring what somebody else drew."

Again the stubborn blue-husky eyes. "What do *you* know?" said Frances. And then, "Can I come with you today to the cliff beach?"

Kate wondered what process of thinking occurred in Frances's head that she could combine an insult and a request in one breath. "No, you can't come," Kate said. "You absolutely can't." And it gave her satisfaction to walk off and leave Frances there amid her rainbow crayons.

"Let's go paint rocks on Saturday," Ian had said. Kate was determined that neither Amanda nor Frances would come along. Ordinarily one or both of them were there, grabbing for the kite string, trying to sing along, teasing Ian to play croquet. It seemed to Kate that when she talked to Ian more times than not it was over the sound of Amanda's voice. But this was Saturday and they were going to the cliff beach and she was damned if the little girls were going to come along.

And they didn't. And it was a beautiful day.

The path down the cliff was steep and narrow. Kate could feel her toes pushing hard against the ends of her sneakers. From high up, the ocean looked streaked—blue, then white where the waves broke, and red along the shore where the clay from the cliffs washed out into the water. Wind swept her hair into her face, flapped at the tails of her shirt. Far out on the water there was a sailboat moving quickly.

She turned to Ian. "Look. You can see the mainland. You hardly ever can." The air was as clear as panes of washed glass and the coast of Massachusetts spread out, hazy in the distance. Ian caught up to her and shaded his eyes like an explorer. "Silent, on a peak in Darien," Kate said.

Ian dropped his hand. "I forget who wrote that."

"Keats. About Cortez discovering the Pacific Ocean and realizing what that meant, how much there was in the world that he hadn't even dreamed of."

Ian smiled at her. "Such erudition."

He was teasing her. Kate liked being teased.

Farther down the cliff she began to run. The grade was so steep it was almost impossible not to. Behind her, pebbles showered down, and she could hear Ian's rubber soles sliding on the loose earth. She jumped the last bit and landed in the sand. They walked down the beach, looking for a place to settle.

The beach was small and, for a Saturday, there weren't many people there. Mostly there were children digging in the clay. A few couples sunned themselves like seals on rocks near the water. Kate leaned back on her towel and closed her eyes and felt the sun on her forehead and eyelids.

"Are we going to paint rocks?" Ian said.

"Do you really want to?"

"I thought that was the reason we came to this beach."

"We'll feel silly."

"Why should we?"

"It's something children do."

"Until now, maybe." He tugged her hand. "Come on. You said you loved it."

Well, and she *had* loved it, a long time ago, but she stood up, half-reluctant.

"You'll have to show me how you do it," Ian said.

Kate made a face at him. "I think you can probably figure it out."

A couple lying side by side propped up and watched them walk toward the water. Then they lay back down, oblivious. Ian stooped at the water's edge and scraped up a great dripping handful of clay. "Here goes," he said, and began to smear clay on the nearest boulder. Kate took her time, looking for a rock with a smooth surface.

She remembered having done this countless times. While the other children plunged in and began to smear clay, she had held back, studying the rocks critically, searching for one whose surface was right. She walked slowly along the shore now, searching. Half-remembering, she made her way to the end of the beach, to the point where the cliffs rose straight out of the water. And there was the rock. Its sheared face fronted on the sea, smoothed by who-knew-how-many years of weathering. It towered above her, enormous still, although she was many times taller than she had been the last time she tried to paint it. Its sheer face was like a wall but she remembered that on its back side there were footholds. She remembered it suddenly in great detail.

For a minute she stood looking at the rock's face, remembering the effort it had taken to work her way even halfway up, and then she scooped up a handful of clay and made a first great swooping curve low down on the smooth surface. The warm rock and the dripping clay and the itch of sand on her palm were so familiar that she might have been nine years old again; nothing changed. And then Kate remembered that the last time she painted the rock she had been twelve, and that she had ruined a new bikini, staining it with clay. She supposed that she had ruined all her bathing suits the years she painted rocks.

She looked down at the suit she wore and thought that she ought to have warned Ian about the lasting effects of the clay on cloth. But then she went back to painting.

She made a series of curves, scooping clay and sweeping it higher on the rock, using the palms of her hands and her fingers like brushes. Water lapped her ankles and the red clay ran down her arms, streaking her with red. She scooped and painted, laying down great overlapping strokes, interlocking curves, spiraling patterns. She did a series of snail whorls that she remembered having seen on a Cretan vase. Then a sort of free-form octopus shape. Shapes and patterns came to her from pictures she'd looked at, from pottery she'd seen in glass cases in echoing museum rooms. She forgot to look around at Ian. She began not to hear the voices of the children on the beach.

Scooping and painting, she made her way around the rock to the rougher side, carried by the momentum of the curving shapes she was painting. The bulging outcroppings of the rock began to dictate shapes to her, and like a cave painter, she began to use these as part of her design. A swoop here. A zigzag there. A free sweep of clay down a crevice. She stood on tiptoe, stretching as far as she could, and made a fat bulge of rock above her into the side of a bison. Clay ran down her body, drying and caking in the wind. She left her own handprints on the rock, as the ancient painters at Lascaux had done.

Finally she had gone as far as she could without climbing. She tipped back her head and looked up. The old footholds were still there—naturally occurring indentations in the rock, just as she remembered them. She scooped handfuls of clay and flung them at the rock above her, spattering herself with red. She scooped and threw until there were mounds of clay clinging to the outcroppings— enough, she judged, to finish the painting. And then she hoisted herself and began to climb.

90

It felt wonderful climbing up into the wind. Her hair snapped against her shoulders. Her feet searched the rock for holds. Her toes dug in, and the rough stone pressed hard against her soles. Her whole body became a brush, bending to scoop the clay she'd thrown. She smeared it in great free whirls across the rock, working her way toward the top.

Far below her, she could see Ian, the couples sunning themselves beside the water, the children running on the sand. She hoisted herself to the top of the rock and clung there, looking far out over the water. She had never made it to the top before. She had never been tall enough before to pull herself up the last several feet.

She felt triumphant. She wanted to keep climbing, to keep painting, to go on and on painting her way into the layers of blue above her. And then she stood up, digging her toes in, balancing on the uneven surface. The wind whipped her hair into streamers behind her. Her eyes stung, but she felt wonderful. She stood fighting the wind like a flag.

Below her, Ian looked up. She waved to him. She waved to the couples on the rocks, semaphoring with her red-stained arms. She wanted to yell. She wanted to make the wild, hoarse, screaming sounds the gulls made. And then, quite suddenly, she wanted to fly.

She leapt straight out, pushing off hard with her feet, and for a miniute it felt like flying. She felt herself plummeting down through the air, and the wind whistling past her. The sand rose toward her. She saw Ian running. She landed. A perfect landing, in a crouch, both feet firmly in the sand.

"My God!" Ian said, "Were you trying to kill yourself?"

Kate rolled over, laughing, in the sand. "No," she said, "I was flying."

Her legs, her arms, her whole body were dyed red and encrusted with sand. Her hair was stiff with clay. She jumped up and began running toward the water. "Come on," she called over her shoulder, "wash off."

She dived into a wave, shot up on the other side. She swam hard a few yards, still feeling the wild, free-fall of her body cutting through thin air. Clay streamed off her just as she remembered. The water around her turned red.

"It never all comes off," she said. "We'll be a little bit this color for a day or two. I forgot to tell you that."

Ian was drying off, streaking the towel. Kate looked at her rock with satisfaction. The clay was nearly dry. Her swoops and curves looked ancient, as if they had been there as long as the rock had.

Ian stretched out on the towel beside her. Kate contentedly poured handfuls of sand over her feet. "Why did you jump off that rock?" he said.

"Felt like it."

"It wasn't a very smart thing to do."

"No," she agreed. She supposed that was true. But she remembered the pure feeling of joy as she sailed through the air, her body like an extension of the curves she had painted.

92

"Well, you did some nice things with the rock," he said, "anyway."

Kate studied the rock. "I kept remembering things I'd seen," she said. "Pictures of cave paintings, pottery designs, all kinds of things." She stretched out her legs and looked at her toes. "Right now I wish I could spend my whole life painting rocks," she said.

"What about just painting?"

Kate glanced at him, lying flat, eyes closed. He was serious. "That's what my father does," she said.

"That's what a lot of people do."

"No, Ian," she said, "I told you a long time ago, I need my own thing."

"Does painting stop being a person's 'own thing' just because other people are also painting?"

"No, of course."

"Well, then?"

Kate curled her toes and said nothing.

12

Certainly Kate was better. She rarely had an afternoon fever. She was sometimes tired, but not *as* tired, and her glands didn't ache at all. It occurred to her that she could probably go to Long Island now if she wanted, but she didn't. She was content—more than content—to be at home. The days drifted by in slow motion. Nothing much happened. Nothing much changed.

There was another professor at lunch one day. Greek salad, French bread, and Professor Kincaid, who began every other sentence by saying "In point of fact."

"Mr. Kincaid is doing an article on my 'August Series.' "

"In point of fact, I have only begun."

Kate smiled a tiny smile at Ian, and pursued an olive around her plate.

Later she took her notebook and her Shakespeare down to the pond. It was a lovely afternoon. Sometime, she thought, she would write an article about the way some of these professors talked. She'd listened to enough of them. And then, suddenly, it came to her that if she kept on with English, she'd probably end up a professor herself. She stared at the pond. The prospect seemed dust-colored on this shimmering afternoon.

She opened her book and began to underline. Leah had said she didn't need to like Prospero to write about him. True. And certainly she had to write. She had to get beyond reading and begin writing this paper.

In bed that morning, she had decided to try writing about the political implications in the play. She thought she would be comfortable doing that. So now she flopped onto her stomach and started thumbing through the pages, under-lining passages that she could discuss from this point of view. Yet all the time her pencil moved, she seemed to hear Mr. Kincaid's voice expressing her thoughts: "One could claim that Prospero represents a type of imperialist. In point of fact, he stole the island from the natives. Indeed, he made them his slaves." Kate tried to imagine a whole life of writing things like that. She closed her eyes and saw colors.

Later she swam. Later still she packed up her books and wandered restlessly up through the meadow. All around her the meadow was in bloom, shades of orange and peach, apricot and yellow, mixing with a hundred shades of green. Frills of Queen Anne's lace, sunlight like syrup, but in her ear Mr. Kincaid's cautious voice went on and on like a droning of gray bees.

In the kitchen she found her mother beating egg whites in a copper bowl. Kate sat down at the kitchen table and leaned on her elbows, looking absently at the bowl in her mother's arm. It made a lovely picture—the green of her mother's shirt, the curve of her arm, the copper, the white froth of the eggs.

"Did you mind very much when you stopped painting?" Kate asked.

"Yes, I minded."

"Was there ever anything else that seemed as good?"

"Lots of things. Painting wasn't exactly pleasure for me, Kate. I wasn't good enough, and I knew I never would be."

"And you've never thought of starting again?"

"Never."

And then her mother stopped whisking and looked at Kate. There was something almost shy in her expression. "I think about the garden a lot," she said. "I think about the colors, what to plant next to what. I flatter myself by thinking that that's a kind of art."

"It's a beautiful garden," Kate said.

"And then there's your father's work. I'm so involved with that."

Kate looked down at the table, studied a dark streak running through the wood. "And that's enough?" she said.

"For me it is. But I never had your talent, Kate."

She was testing the egg whites, making small mountain

peaks with the whisk. "We weren't talking about me," Kate said.

"Oh," said her mother. "That's what I thought you were getting at."

Her paints were not in the attic. She had been sure she'd left them there. It seemed ironic that, out of this welter of objects that never were discarded, her paints should have disappeared. Maybe they were only buried, she thought, under the slowly accreting mountain of things there under the roof, but she couldn't find them and it was too hot to stay long looking.

There was a school child's box of watercolors lying on the floor together with a pad of cheap paper. Kate stooped to pick them up. Old and dry and never very good to begin with, the paints were good enough for her purposes, she thought. They'd do. Probably they had belonged to Amanda, who never painted much. The paints, though old, were scarcely touched and the brushes were like new.

Just for fun, Kate told herself. Nothing serious. That was why she'd gone up to find paints in the first place. That was why, the next afternoon, she sat beside the pond, dipping a brush into the water, trying to moisten one of the dry cakes of paint.

When Ian came down for his swim and saw what she was doing, he laughed at her. "That's like trying to ski on barrel staves," he said. "Why don't you get yourself some decent colors?"

Kate shrugged. "I'm just playing."

"Is that right?" said Ian. "Just painting another rock or two, are you?"

She looked up at him. "Well, what do you think I'm doing?"

"I think you're doing something you've been wanting to do all summer, and I think it's crazy to do it with those rotten paints."

And it seemed that, next, they were driving into town. Kate didn't remember how that had happened or what he had said, or whether he'd really said much of anything at all. It was simply agreed that she needed better colors, and then they were in the car, driving.

They drove to the only store on the island that sold anything worth buying. Kate had been there often before, of course, and she merely said, "Turn here" and "Down this street" and "There it is on the corner."

And then they were in the store itself, and it smelled exactly as Kate remembered. The bare wood floors were the same, too, and the glass counters, and the paints, and pastels and tablets of heavy paper.

"Look," Kate said. "That's the kind of watercolors I used to have. I'll bet they cost a fortune."

Ian leaned against the glass case and they looked down at the display together. "I doubt I can afford them," said Kate.

"They'd be worth it, though. They're the best."

They asked to see them.

To Kate, even the outsides of the tubes were beautiful. She remembered the feel of a tube in her hand, its weight and its resiliency. She remembered that as a child she had opened a new box of paints with held breath, with a shiver of pleasure. She felt that now, opening the wooden box, picking up a tube and holding it in her hand. It resisted the slight pressure of her thumb and forefinger as though it contained something alive. "Aren't they lovely?" she said to Ian, and he nodded. He looked them over carefully, as if he, too, knew how it felt to enjoy even their outsides, even their labels.

"Yes," he said finally, "they really are lovely. You'll have to afford them."

They were just as expensive as Kate had known they would be. They cost all of what she had left from her last summer's job and then some, and so Ian lent her the extra money. And then, while she was telling him that he shouldn't, he bought her some good heavy paper as well.

They rode home with the package between them, and it seemed to Kate that Ian was as pleased as she was. "I'll pay you back," she said. "As soon as I can."

Ian said, "No hurry."

And they rode along with their brown-paper package, and sang about chain gangs in Tennessee.

There was so much she had forgotten! Simple things. And there were other things she wondered if she ever had known. The more she painted, the more this bothered her, and she had begun to paint every day.

In the morning she lay in bed and looked at the trees outside framed by her window. Simple enough—two green trees separated by a patch of sky. It was a view she saw every morning, but when she tried to paint it, she couldn't get it right.

Worse than this were figures. She looked at her mother sitting in a beach chair—a sling of red canvas, a circle of straw. She wanted to paint her exactly as she saw her, but later, working from memory, she couldn't.

A group of tourists she saw in town, Amanda and a friend from camp squatting on the grass, plump and flushed as Renoir children—none of it looked on paper the way she thought it should. It seemed that the distance between what she could see and what she could do grew wider as she worked, and it was a special kind of sadness to her that this should be so.

She wondered how she had ever painted the picture in the closet, and in oils. She felt clumsy as a child with the watercolors now. But Ian kept saying, "Give yourself time. You're just starting."

Beside the pond she crumpled up a failure. "Go easy on that paper," Ian said. He was stretched out on the bank, reading. His back looked polished, smooth and brown, glossy as taffy. He was proud of his tan because, as he had told her, red-haired people didn't tan much, and this represented some magical turn of events.

"God," she'd said, "you sound like Leah." But she liked his tan, too. She would have liked to paint it.

She squinted her eyes and looked at the color and at the curve of his shoulders, and at his ribs, each separate and distinct as ridged sand. She imagined the picture as a series of smooth, shallow curves, the colors of sand and melted brown sugar.

"I'm trying to go easy on this paper," she said. "But I should have started with something cheaper. This is too good for what I can do."

Then she stood up and walked over to where he was lying. She could smell the humid, brackish water and the odor of crushed grass. She knelt beside him and sat back on her heels. "I can't believe how much technique I've lost."

"Maybe that isn't it. Maybe you're trying to do things you haven't done before."

Kate thought there was some truth in this. "I never did do figures much," she said. And why would she have? Her father didn't do figures—or hadn't for a very long time.

"All the same," she said, "the problem remains. I don't know enough."

"You aren't being very efficient you know." Ian rolled over and squinted up at her. "You have one of the really great painters in this country about a hundred yards up the path. Why not ask him for some help?"

"Oh," Kate said. She shrugged. "I want to paint my own kind of thing."

"You don't have to paint exactly like someone else to learn from him, you know."

And again Kate shrugged. There wasn't much more she could say. The one subject that was off-limits between them was her father. Things she could tell Leah she could not say to him.

101

"It might be a good thing for both of you," Ian said. "He's feeling pretty low about his own work right now. You might take his mind off it."

Kate thought that it was some measure of Ian's generosity that he imagined generosity everywhere. The idea that her father couldn't be bothered was something Ian would find hard to understand. And so she said, "Well, if I did that, you might not have to listen to so many of his stories."

"I like listening to his stories. Can you imagine what an opportunity that is for a lowly graduate student in the history of art?"

"No doubt fantastic," Kate replied and began to ease herself into the water.

"Well, it is, you know."

The more she painted, the more she longed to learn. Several times more, Ian suggested asking her father for help. Now and then Kate felt tempted to explain to him how impossible she would find that, but always she stopped herself before she began.

She began to look at some of the paintings in the house more closely, though. The painting above the mantel, for instance. A dab of color, a streak, and a whole three-dimensional shape resulted. How? Kate wondered. She looked.

Even the great self-insisting whirls of color in his later work, the arrogant jutting verticals of his "August Series," which she had never liked, she looked at now because they could teach her something. She studied the way he had applied the paint, what he had done with line.

Little by little, some of Ian's respect for her father's work infected her. He was a great painter. No matter what else she felt about him, she had to concede that.

Bits of things she had watched him do or had asked him to explain began coming back to her. Almost every day she remembered something. From him she had absorbed some idea about how to handle paints, about how to organize a composition and achieve balance. These things were stored inside her, she discovered, preserved from years before.

She kept painting.

13

One morning, a crash overhead. Kate was awake instantly, her first thought being that Mrs. Hilmer had gone mad and was cleaning the attic.

Another crash and the sound of something heavy being dragged across the floor. Kate jumped up and reached for her robe. She tiptoed across the hall to the attic door and looked up into the dusty twilight. The space at the head of the stairs was blocked by cartons. And then Ian appeared, arms full of boxes, only his head and shoulders visible above the pile.

"What are you *doing* up there?" Kate said.

"Did I wake you up? I'm sorry."

"But what are you doing?"

"Someplace up here your father thinks there are preliminary drawings for some of his paintings. I'm trying to find them."

Remembering her own experiences in the attic, Kate said, "You never will."

"Yes, I will. If they're here, I will."

"Maybe, if you have a month to spend." And then, "Do you want some help?"

Of course he wanted help. She went to dress quickly.

The attic was stifling. Ian's efforts had already raised dust that hung in the air in a sort of unmoving fog. Festoons of cobwebs dangled from the rafters, getting caught in Kate's hair. The clean shirt she'd put on was already streaked with dirt and clinging to her back.

"What makes you think they're up here?" she said.

"Nothing, except that they aren't in the studio, and this is the only place your father can think of."

"And you need them."

"Well, of course I need them. Part of the exhibit's going to be devoted to preliminary drawings."

He was in no mood to chat. They opened carton after carton—baby clothes, worn-out toys, back issues of *Artnews*, scraps of fabric from curtains that had worn out years ago. They went through the drawers of old files, looking into every folder. They lifted boxes down from shelves, dumped the contents, sorted, repacked. After a while Kate began to think it was funny.

"If we died up here," she said, "they'd look five years before they found our skeletons in this mess."

Ian said, "Keep looking."

They worked their way around the room systematically, ducking under the sloping ceiling to reach into the corners. They climbed over old mattresses, over lopsided wicker chairs, rolled rugs, broken lamps. "Almost everything up here is familiar to me," Kate said. "It's like reliving the past." And when Ian didn't reply, she said, "That's Amanda's crib, for instance. I can remember when she used to try to put her head through the slats."

Ian, going through desk drawers, grunted.

"Can't you imagine the way she looked trying to stick her head through them?"

"Funny, I guess."

"Yes, funny." Kate was beginning to feel cross. "I can't believe a few drawings are all that important," she said. "I think the world might survive without them."

No reply. More drawers opening. More suitcases ransacked.

"Well, I'm not going to look anymore," she said.

She went down to the kitchen to make them iced tea and climbed back up the attic stairs with the rattling glasses. "Do you think you could stop long enough to drink this?" she asked.

They sat in two of the wicker chairs under the dangling cobwebs. Ian surveyed the room. "That's mother's painting over there," Kate said. "The big square thing wrapped in sheets." And then, "Want to see it?"

"Yes. Sure." He wasn't thinking about what she'd said. Nevertheless, Kate decided to unwrap it.

Getting to it was almost a journey, across piles of old

furniture, around ratty hanging garment bags. She wondered why she was bothering, since she'd seen the picture many times and Ian didn't seem really interested. Still, she lifted the painting away from the wall and pulled off the sheets around it. "There. Can you see?"

He nodded.

"So what do you think?"

"Enormous, isn't it? Your family buys canvas by the acre. If the drawings were that size, we'd have found them hours ago."

"Yes, but what do you *think?*"

She leaned the picture against a box and came around to look for herself. It confused her to see how different it seemed from the painting she remembered. Areas of color. Nice color. Abstract. But what?

"It doesn't look like Mother, does it?" she asked.

"Nothing like her." A joke.

"I mean you'd never guess she was the artist. Or you wouldn't be sure. With my father's pictures, you're always sure. That's one thing about them."

Ian nodded. "What you mean is that it looks like a lot of people's paintings. Any number of people could have done it."

"Derivative?" Kate said.

"Or just young. Uncertain. Learning."

"Except she wasn't so young," Kate said. "She was thirty. She'd been painting a long time."

"Thirty isn't so old," Ian said. And then he stood up and started rummaging again. Kate wrapped the painting in its sheets, being careful because the paint was dry and cracking.

Later—much later—Ian found the drawings in a file drawer. "So you see," he said, "it was worth the effort." And then he was chatty again, happy, shoving things back into some approximation of order, but Kate was still half-mad at him.

"I feel as if I'd had a tour of the Brewer family history," he said.

"That's what I was trying to tell you when you weren't listening," she said.

They shoved the last few boxes away from the stairs. Ian gathered up the drawings carefully, and they started down.

The downstairs hall seemed twenty degrees cooler—almost air conditioned. Kate shut the attic door. "Is your painting someplace up there, too?" Ian asked. "The one that won the prize?"

"No. It's in my closet."

"Can I see it?"

Kate hesitated.

"Don't want to show me?" he asked.

"I don't think so. Not now."

But then, when he was already halfway across the yard, heading for the studio, Kate leaned out her window and called, "All right. If you really want to see it." And he looked up and came back. And Kate had the picture out and unwrapped by the time he had come upstairs.

He put the drawings on the bed, and leaned against the

bedpost. Kate watched his face closely. "Oh," he said. And his face was such a strange mixture of things that Kate could tell nothing.

She made a move toward the picture. "Don't," he said. "Let me look for a minute." And then finally, "It's good, Kate. It's just very, very good."

She took a breath. She grinned. And suddenly she wanted to talk. "You see why I've been complaining about what I've forgotten? I really did know more then."

And, "The light. Do you think it works? Do you like it? And the sky? Remember when I told you I thought skies were hard? They are, but I think I was working out a way to handle skies here."

And, "I don't know why I didn't want you to see it. Yes, I do. I was afraid you wouldn't like it."

"How could I not like it?"

"Does the composition seem right to you? Balanced? What do you think? I was worried about whether I should have arranged things differently."

On and on she went, and Ian kept nodding or shaking his head, as if he knew that she didn't really want answers, but only to talk. Which was what she did want. She had waited a long time to talk about this painting.

"You see, I wanted to get the light that you see in the meadow early in the morning. That was the main thing. I always loved the way the studio looked in that light. But now I wonder. Maybe I sacrificed balance for light?"

"Oh, no," Ian said. "It's fine."

* * *

Later Kate stopped for a minute at the storeroom door. "You really did like it, didn't you?" she said.

"Kate, yes."

"You wouldn't be saying that only to be kind?"

"No."

"Would you know it was *my* painting?"

"Yes. I can't imagine that particular painting being anyone else's."

"What do you mean?"

"There's a lot of passion in that painting, Kate. That's what comes through. It's really kind of overwhelming."

"So you really like it?"

Ian sat back in his chair and looked at her. "How many more ways can I say it?" he said. "I like the painting. It's wonderful."

When Kate made no move to leave, he set some file cards to one side and looked at her. "When my sister was a little girl," he said, "she had a couple of questions she used to ask me over and over. I can't remember what they were, though God knows why not. One day I wrote down the answers on a sheet of paper and told her that any time she wanted the answers, to read them from then on. Want me to do that for you?"

Kate shook her head. "No. I just want to be sure you really mean what you're saying."

Ian groaned. "How many more times do you want to hear it?"

On the other side of the screen door, Kate simply stood there, smiling.

"I can't believe it," Kate said. *"There can't be more miss-*ing. How can he have been so careless?"

"Well, he thinks these are in a collection in Boston. He's lost the records. I'm checking."

Kate was floating in the pond. The water was like soup. The air was like soup. She was perfectly happy.

"My family is beginning to wonder if I'm ever coming home," he said. "They hadn't expected I'd be gone so long."

"It's because everything here is so mixed-up and con-fused," Kate said. And felt glad for the confusion.

She wondered if he had begun to talk of home more, or if she just imagined that he had. She didn't ask him about California any longer. She had forgotten the names of his brother and sister, had forgotten the name of the town in the California hills where he lived, as if, by forgetting, she could cancel their reality.

"There have been fires in the hills behind the house," he said.

"Dangerous ones?"

"Sometimes they can be. Sometimes we have to run sprinklers along the property line at the end of the summer."

Her arms and legs felt light as petals. She stirred the smooth brown surface of the water with her hands, sending ripples skating away on either side. "You should have been in town with me this morning," she said. "It looks like a festival. Hundreds of people for the regatta tomorrow. Boats all over the harbor." She watched the silky rippling in the water. "Tonight they have a sort of celebration. Fireworks in the harbor, that kind of thing."

"Is this an interesting bit of local lore you're telling me about, or are you suggesting that we go?"

Kate laughed, turning her head in the water to see him. Then she splashed him, using the flat of her hand, sending a thin wall of water shooting towards him. "I meant, shall we go?"

"If you're going to the fireworks, I'm coming," said Amanda.

"You can't. They'll last too late." Kate had washed her hair and was drying it. It flew out around her in long dark feathers.

"Mother said I could go."

"You're lying, Amanda. She'd never let you stay out that late when you've got camp tomorrow."

"Want to bet?" Amanda said. "Ask her."

Amanda sat in the back seat like a chaperone.

"She'll fall asleep halfway through," Kate said.

"That's all right," said Ian, "I can carry her." And they rode the rest of the way to town listening to Amanda singing.

They found a place to sit on a garage roof overlooking the harbor where they would have a good view of the display. On the eve of the regatta no one's roof or wall was private, and people scrambled up everywhere for the view. Ian went off to buy them ice cream cones, and came back with the cones already dripping. Midway through hers, Amanda fell asleep, collapsing against Ian's knee with a melting glob of chocolate on her cheek. Kate picked up the cone and wiped Amanda, and she and Ian shared the remains while they waited for the dark.

"I knew she wouldn't last," Kate said. "It was ridiculous to bring her."

Crowds of people passed below them—sunburned mostly, in shorts and shifts, some with babies strapped to their backs in slings, some pulling small children by the hand, some still wearing sunglasses as if they hadn't left the beach.

Little by little the darkness settled, coming, it seemed to Kate, like a cloud across the water, narrowing and narrowing the light until there was no light left. Then the first rocket lifted out of the dark, an arrow of light streaking into the dark blue sky.

Kate watched the orange tail shooting upward, and then the burst—small petals of white, then larger petals exploding until the sky overhead was filled with a loose chrysanthemum of light. Everywhere there were gasps, as if no one had ever seen a rocket burst before, or as if the gasps were part of the burst itself. The white petals curved down the sky and fell toward the harbor, falling like stars. And then there was another soft explosion of sound and another orange tail streaking upward.

Amanda's face glowed, chocolate-smeared, in the burst of light. She stirred and grunted. "Maybe we should wake her," Ian said.

"She'll just be grouchy. She's seen fireworks a million times," Kate said.

"It's beautiful to see them over water," said Ian. "I hadn't thought what it would be like—the burst itself and then the reflection, like two displays."

"I've never seen them any other way," Kate said. "They do them over the river in Boston."

"I've seen them all kinds of ways," Ian said. "I remember once my brother got hold of some Roman candles—I don't know how—and we took them up into the hills behind the house and set them off. It was about this time of year and the hills were dry. The first rocket started a fire, of course."

"How old were you?" Kate asked.

"Oh, little. Maybe six or seven. And I was scared. Here

114

was this fire and my brother trying to stamp it out. He sent me down the hill to bring a bucket of water. I remember I never ran so fast in my life. I filled a bucket and started running back up the hill, and naturally the bucket was too heavy for me and I spilled it. God, I was scared. I thought the whole hill would burn. Maybe the whole town."

"What *did* happen?"

"Oh, my brother stamped it out. It wasn't a big fire. It only seemed big to me. I was just a little kid."

Above them a rocket burst, showering light. Kate looked at Ian's face. Far away in some other time he had spilled water, been afraid. There was a family and dry brown hills, and none of it had anything to do with her. She watched the brightness explode and dwindle on his face, lights reflecting in his eyes as if his eyes were harbors. She looked hard, fixing him there beside her on the roof of the garage, making time stop and space scatter like particles of falling light.

All week long Kate painted bursts of light—incandescent flowers above dark water, streaks of orange against a velvet sky.

There were hundreds, perhaps thousands, of fireflies in the grass at night. Amanda went running after them with a jar. Kate and Ian sat on the lawn and watched her white shirt flickering in the darkness at the edge of the meadow.

Kate pulled a blade of grass and nibbled the end, sucking the summer taste of it. Amanda came slowly up the lawn with her jar of phosphorescence. She held it close to Ian's face. "The light," she said, "is on their bottoms. If you want, I can probably collect a jarful for you to take back to California."

Ian explained that it was against the law to take bugs into California. Kate looked at the winking grass, and remembered bursting rockets.

Twice on weekends they went to the beach, walking for miles, collecting shells and bits of sea-polished glass. Amanda ran back and forth between them, but Kate hardly noticed she was there.

One morning Kate drove to town in a downpour. In the afternoon, the path through the meadow was still wet. A grasshopper, landing on a stalk of Queen Anne's lace, shook down a shower of raindrops. Kate stopped to look, fascinated by this little rainbow sprinkle.

As a child, she had known the meadow in this kind of tiny detail. She had studied the dots on ladybugs' wings, the delicate beards of grass seed, the bellies of fireflies, the design of anthills. Looking at the grasshopper's small shower, she was, like a child, content in the present.

Evenings now they flew the kite or sang or watched Amanda catching bugs. When the kite dipped in the evening sky, Kate looked at Ian, looking up. She watched him swim across the pond, walk up through the meadow, butter his toast. She made a hundred drawings in her mind of the angle of his shoulders, the shape of his chin. She imagined painting the terra-cotta of his hair, the white spaces between his fingers when he spread his hand. She learned him in the way she had once learned the meadow, in the smallest, most particular detail—the frayed edge of his shirt sleeve, the crease of his elbow, the squinting lines at the corners of his eyes.

Once she had asked her mother how a person knew when she loved someone. She hadn't meant the family kind of love, but the other kind that she strangely imagined and sometimes thought about. Ten years old, leaning against her mother, she'd asked, and her mother had said, "You'll know."

And that was true, Kate thought. She knew. She had known for quite a while. It hadn't come to her at any one time or in any special place as she had expected, but so slowly that she had hardly recognized its coming at all. It had been there before she gave it a name. Like air, it had been all around her.

When Kate thought about the summer later, it was these days that she remembered best—two weeks like two halves of a hinged shell, enclosing a quiet space in the middle of August. They moved as slowly as days move for a child. The sun crossed the meadow. Fireflies winked after dark at the edge of the lawn. A grasshopper jumped and shook down rain. And at night, leaning against the frame of her window, Kate said the word aloud to herself for the pure pleasure of saying it, listening to the lovely, liquid opening of the vowel, and the v that closed and contained it.

15

Worried letters kept arriving from Leah. They weren't meant to sound worried—just the opposite—but Kate knew her too well to be deceived. They came on green paper, blue paper, sometimes on yellow legal sheets and Kate could see that Leah was on a kind of crusade to cheer her up.

The latest one was typical. "My father is being terrible," Leah wrote. "He says I have to stop buying clothes. With my own money! Can you believe it? What gets into them— fathers?"

Kate dropped the letter onto the ground beside her. She would have to write Leah and tell her not to worry, even if this meant shattering Leah's illusions about her subtlety. She'd tell her that things were not so bad. She'd mention that she was painting.

Then she turned back to her Shakespeare, but only for

a moment. Her mind wouldn't focus on the play. Her eyes wandered from the lines, and she saw Ian coming up through the meadow. Kate marked her place in the book with a blade of grass and watched him. Pushing through the stalks of Queen Anne's lace that grew almost to his waist, skirting the border of her mother's flower bed, he looked so beautiful to Kate that she caught her breath.

In his arms he was carrying two parcels wrapped in brown paper, and when he called, "Do you want to ride into town?" Kate put her book down on the wooden step and followed him to the barn.

"I've got to mail these," he said. "And I told your mother that as long as I was going to be in town, I'd wait to pick up Amanda."

He dumped the packages into the back. Kate climbed into the front seat beside him. The car was warm. Across the road a mowing machine was working in the field. When she cranked down her window, she let in the smell of fresh-cut grass, and Ian said, "In California everything is so brown by now you'd think it was dead." Smelling, Kate thought, the damp, green odor, too.

"The chrysanthemums have begun to bloom," she said. She had noticed them in the garden that morning.

"Are those the little yellow flowers?"

"And white," she said, "and bronze." But that wasn't the point. The chrysanthemums were autumn flowers. The summer was nearly over.

She sat in the car while he mailed the packages, and studied his back on the other side of the post office's plate glass window. The summer was nearly over; the word she had been hoarding to herself had to be said soon if it was going to be said at all. And the idea of saying it scared her.

Kate looked at the old car's raveling visor, its chipped dashboard, its ripped seat. Then she looked at Ian, working his way to the front of the line. She had never told anyone that she loved him before. Well, she'd never *loved* anyone before. The risk had always seemed too great.

She had lost track of Ian's shirt and saw for a moment only the tired signs in the post office window advertising rummage sales and Memorial Day parades. And then she saw him coming toward the door, and she thought that whatever was going to happen was beginning now.

He leaned into the window of the car. "Do you want a Coke or something? We've got some time to wait for Amanda's bus."

Kate slid across the seat under the steering wheel and climbed out. They walked down the main street, looking in windows, and stopped to buy lemonade at an outdoor stand. They sat on a bench that faced the harbor. The wood was hot on Kate's bare legs.

A boat with sails furled was motoring into the harbor. Around them there was bustle—a group of kids checking in rental bikes, dogs nosing at the waste cans, a truck backing slowly up an alley behind them—but Kate felt suspended in stillness. "I'm going to miss all this," Ian said.

Kate nodded. "You're almost finished, aren't you?" she said. "That's why you mailed the boxes. They're full of your notes."

"Most of my notes. What's left I can take with me in the car."

For weeks and weeks, she had known this time was coming. She had been putting it out of her mind.

"When do you think you'll be going?" she asked.

"About a week. I have to go to Boston and track down those drawings. Then I'll come back and finish up."

Kate looked down at her cup of shaved ice. She finished the last of the lemonade and wadded up her napkin and held it crumpled in her hand. She watched a boat maneuvering between the other boats moored in the harbor. "When are you going up to Boston?" she asked. He told her, and she nodded. She watched the boat sliding slowly past another, and before it had cleared that boat's stern, she knew what she was going to do.

Amanda talked all the way home. Kate hadn't any idea what she was talking about and didn't care. She let Ian answer the questions that needed answering. She watched the summer fields glide by.

The mower had finished in the field across the road. There was a blackbird sitting on the ridgepole of the house, a basket of weeds in the driveway. Amanda kept talking right into the barn.

Kate followed her into the house, coming up the porch

steps behind the thudding camp bag. There was a note about dinner on the kitchen table. She had forgotten her parents were going out.

She put a casserole into the oven, made a salad. The three of them took their plates outside and ate on the grass in the shade beside the porch. Afterwards Amanda wanted to fly the kite, but Ian had work to do.

"You hardly ever work after dinner," Amanda protested.

"But tonight I have to," he said. "I'm going up to Boston tomorrow."

Kate washed the dishes by herself. She offered and Amanda didn't object. Later she supervised Amanda's bath and read her a story and tucked her in bed. Then she brushed her hair before the mirror in her room—long, slow strokes without hurry. She turned on the lights in the sitting room and, after that, she started down through the meadow.

She moved with a kind of slow certainty, the way she had sometimes moved in dreams. It seemed to her that all around her things had slowed, that she was swimming through time as if it were still water.

The grass was yellow in the evening light. It was wet on the soles of her feet. A bobwhite called plaintively from someplace at the fringes of the meadow. There was a moon, a chalky crescent, high above the studio roof.

Ian was working in the studio itself, checking files there. His back was turned to the door. Kate stood a minute, hesitating, and then she knocked and went in.

He was surprised. "Is Amanda okay?" He said it as if he thought that the only thing that could bring her here was an emergency.

"Yes. She's asleep. Or at least she's in bed." He waited, and Kate saw that he was wondering what she was there for.

Above her she saw the moon through the skylight. Through the windows she could see the meadow growing dim. The gooseneck lamp shining on the files where he was working made the only small light in the room.

She had no preamble. She hadn't tried to think of one. She looked once around the room, so utterly familiar, and then she looked at him and pushed off into thin air.

"Ian," she said, "take me with you to Boston."

This was all she said, but it seemed to take a long time. There were wide spaces between the words, gaps big enough to fall through. The sentence was like a journey undertaken, miles between its beginning and its end, and when it was finished, Kate stared at the floor. All around her there was silence.

When finally she raised her head to look at him, Ian said simply, "Oh, Kate."

His face was expressionless, as blank as any face she had ever seen. She stood waiting, but she saw there was nothing to wait for. Everything she needed to know was written there where nothing was written. It was as if she had entered into a bad old dream.

Ian started to speak. Kate shook her head. "Don't," she

said. "You don't have to say anything. I know what you'll say. You're here to do my father's cataloging. That has nothing to do with me."

Her sentence had been the journey, she thought. All the journey that there was going to be. She had put out her hand, and he was moving away. He seemed to be dissolving before her, but it might be, Kate thought, that this was because there were tears in her eyes.

"Kate," he said, "look." But how could she look? "You're right," he said, as she knew she was. "I am here to do your father's cataloging, which is one of the reasons I can't take you."

Kate looked at the floor, trying to make the tears that filled her eyes retreat. "It wouldn't be fair to your father," Ian said. "It wouldn't be the right thing to do."

Kate nodded, looking hard at the old paint-spattered floorboards.

"But—," Ian began, and she shook her head. She couldn't bear to be there any longer, in that room where now there was nothing but sadness and the memory of sadness, and so she turned and ran, stumbling out the door and up the meadow path, clumsy as a child, sick with humiliation.

She plunged through the kitchen door, through the dark kitchen into the sitting room where there was light. The picture above the mantel shone in the lamplight—the table, the cat, the chair, and the child.

Kate saw the painting through a blur of tears. She leaned against the mantel and sobbed, feeling the hard wooden edge of it gouging her shoulder. The pain seemed to go

124

down and down inside her like a rock finding its way to the bottom of a well.

It felt to her as if this had all happened before, and would happen and happen as long as she lived. Everything she had ever cared about belonged to her father—his to give and his to take away.

Above her the painting swam, losing focus, becoming only colors inhabiting space.

16

In the morning she stayed in her room. She heard the car go, but she didn't watch it go. She listened to it pulling hard up the hill to the county road. She imagined the curving strip of blacktop before it, and the ferry swallowing it into its dark hold.

There was no point trying to work or to paint. During the two days Ian was gone, Kate wasn't sure what she did at all. Mostly she tried to think how it would be when he returned, what she could say, what he would say, how they could possibly behave now with one another.

Going to Boston with him? What had she meant that to mean? She picked at the hem of her bedspread. She divided a blade of grass with her nail. She sat staring at the mucky bottom of the pond. She had meant it to mean whatever it *would* mean, whatever being two days and nights with him meant. It had been her way of saying she loved him.

He knew that. It would be as hard for him as for her to sit at the table and pretend that she had never asked him to take her to Boston. She tried to imagine how they would put in the few days remaining, how they would avoid being at the same time in the same room, but her imagination snagged on this problem again and again, snagged on the sharp edge of wanting to be with him.

When he came back, Kate was in town, having driven in to drop off her mother. Coming home, she saw the old car when she reached the top of the hill, and she felt suddenly hollow, a cave of air.

She parked the car and crossed the lawn. She supposed that he had gone directly to the studio. She sat on a stool in the kitchen and watched a fly—a fat summer fly—crawling up the window screen. It would be good to be a fly, she thought, crawling up a screen, circling the rim of a jam jar. Simple, and safe, and unconscious—satisfied with an atom of jam.

And while she was thinking this, she saw Ian coming up through the meadow.

There was a laundry bag slung over his shoulder, and it seemed to Kate that he was moving toward her faster than she could comprehend what was happening. It was like a film running through at high speed. He was in the meadow, then on the lawn, and then on the porch before she could even put her feet on the floor. And then he was there, through the back door, swinging his bag off his shoulder.

"I was wondering where everyone was," he said.

Kate took a breath.

"I came up to do some laundry."

And then he was on his way down the cellar steps. She heard his feet on the stairs, and the door of the washer opening. He called to ask her if they were out of soap, and Kate found herself standing at the head of the stairs telling him where to look for more. It seemed to her that none of this could be happening.

"The entire ferry was full of Girl Scouts," he called.

"With bikes?"

"Right. There must have been a few hundred." And then, "God, it was hot and miserable in Boston. You'd have hated it."

It was like a gift, she thought, like some kind of present. If she tried imagining for a year, she would never have guessed that it was going to be like this, the two of them yelling up and down a flight of wooden steps about laundry and Girl Scouts, and, just as casually, about going to Boston.

The washer went into action—a preliminary roar, and then the sound of water—and Ian was coming up the steps again. "I brought you something from there," he said. He was fumbling in the pocket of his shirt.

"I found it in the museum shop," he said. "It's a picture of a rabbit."

Kate held out her hand. Before she looked, she knew

what it would be. She turned the postcard over and saw the sunny field with its daubs of red paint, and then she looked up and saw Ian.

"I thought you'd like to have it."

"Yes," she said.

In the cellar, the washer changed cycles. He put his arms around her, and she knew that he had begun to talk. It was odd, Kate thought, that it was possible to know that someone was talking when you didn't hear a word he said. She felt the strange curve of his arms around her, and the way that her shoulders fitted into the curve.

Someplace in the house Mrs. Hilmer was battering a room into order, but Kate didn't care. She hardly heard, absorbed in this melting feeling, no longer sure which was his body and which was hers.

After a while, she began to listen to what he was saying, listening vaguely. "I'd have liked to take you, Kate," he said, "But I'm too old for you right now. I have to go too far away."

She knew the kinds of things he must have been saying before. She understood what he was saying now. But the palm of his hand was on the crown of her head and his fingers were in her hair. Between the pale spaces of his spread hand, she imagined her dark hair.

He was telling her that he was going away. But his hand was telling her that it was not because he didn't care for her. His hand was stroking the long, straight length of her hair, and was telling her that she was beautiful.

"This isn't the right time, Kate," he said, "or the right

circumstance. But here and now aren't all that there will ever be for you."

Still, Kate thought, here and now were all there would ever be of *this,* and so she rested against him and felt his hand curve over the curve of her skull, and down along the nape of her neck, and over the hair on her shoulders. And she thought of Miranda, gazing for the first time on all the shipwrecked men, the first besides her father that she had ever seen.

"And so—," Ian said.

"Don't talk anymore," said Kate. "I understand you."

And then they just stood there, while below them the washer sloshed and above them Mrs. Hilmer ran the vacuum, and Kate held her postcard and leaned against Ian, and Ian stroked her hair.

On the day that Ian left there was the first cool smell of fall in the air in the early morning. Kate put on a sweater before she came down to breakfast, and she hugged it around her while she watched him pack the car.

Everyone came out to see him off. Even if they had wanted to, there was no time or chance then to say more than they had already said, but there was nothing left that needed saying. "Now and here aren't all that there will ever be," he had said. There were numbers of ways that she could choose to interpret that, and Kate chose to let it stand that way, with many meanings.

She stood beside the mailbox and watched him drive away. The car raised a cloud of dust in the morning air.

She watched until the dust had settled, and then she went back to the house.

Her mother was in the kitchen, rinsing breakfast dishes. Kate stood at the table, and handed her plates. "I meant to give Ian some beach plum jelly to take along," her mother said. "I'm sure that's something they don't have in California."

"They have beaches. Why not beach plums?"

"I think the vegetation in California must be different." It was the sort of conversation that she and her mother sometimes had, not so much for the sake of what they said, but because their voices moving back and forth were a kind of touching.

After they had finished with the dishes, they sat at the kitchen table, drinking coffee, and they didn't talk at all. Then her mother took her hand and held it, as she sometimes had done when Kate was a child, and they sat and listened to a bobwhite calling for his mate in the meadow, his voice as clear and insistent as a flute.

17

There was a road crew patching holes in front of the house.
In the downstairs hall, Frances Hilmer was swinging on
the newel post. Leah's latest letter declared that she was
no longer in love. "The creep!" she wrote. "It turned out
he has the brains of a Neanderthal. I realized I was talking
all summer to a rock. *Why* did I waste my time on him?"

Things had a way of getting on, Kate thought. All the
little daily things kept right on happening, pushing her
along.

"You slept late," Frances said in a conversational way,
as Kate passed her on the stairs.

"So what?" Kate said and slammed out the screen door.

She pulled a chair around to the side of the house and
sat down. Her paper was one of the daily things pushing
her to get on, and wearily she opened her notebook. After

a while Frances went by with her crayons. Kate studied her small retreating back and wondered how anyone could love a child like that. Then she lay back in the chair and looked at the wall of the house, mainly because she didn't feel like looking at Frances.

High above a jet streaked the sky, going west. Kate wondered where Ian might be at that moment. She thought of his worn old car with its ragged visors, and of him, squinting at the road, miles and miles away now, going west.

The jet trail dissolved slowly above her, and it seemed to Kate that the edge of the house was dissolving, too, the gray of the shingles melting into the blue of the sky along a hairline of reflected color. Even as she watched, the light changed, and the shingles modulated from a cool to a yellower gray. If she were going to paint that wall, she thought, she would have to find a way to suggest that modulation, that dissolution of the solid edge into the transparency of the sky. She wished sharply, terribly that Ian were there at that minute to talk to about this.

"How come you're doing that with your eyes?" Frances asked. Kate started, and looked into her damp and solid face.

"Are you planning to stand there?" Kate said. "Because if you are, I think I'll probably move."

"But why *are* you?" Frances repeated.

"Because I was noticing some things about that wall." Kate pointed. "You could probably spend your whole life painting the way the color changes."

Frances turned, blank as a toad. "What for?"

"You mean why would you do it?" Kate paused. "Well, because it would be interesting. It's an interesting problem."

Frances appeared unconvinced. "Your whole life?" she said.

"You could," Kate said. "And then some."

"Your whole life is all there is," Frances said. "There isn't any 'then some.' "

"Okay. You're right. There isn't."

"Except in heaven."

"Right, Frances. You're absolutely right. Now go, okay?"

Frances burped, the sound maneuvering its way through a series of gurgles until it arrived in her throat. "Excuse me," she said.

"Are you going?" Kate asked.

Frances gave her a cold stare. "My mother says you're just like your father," she said. "She says your mother is the only person in your family who even cares a little bit about how other people feel."

Kate doubted Mrs. Hilmer had ever said such a thing. She thought that Frances had probably invented it that minute. But then, "My mother says you're so mean and selfish you won't even ask him about my oil picture." Frances produced this triumphantly, and then, hoisting her coloring book onto her hip, she went.

Kate watched her going. Then she looked at the wall again, and at all of the cool, theoretical problems contained there. A person could spend a lifetime, she thought again,

134

painting nothing but those fifteen feet of shingles. And then, like Frances, she thought, What for?

Frances was almost at the barn. Kate had to raise her voice to be heard. She called, "Come here, Frances."

Frances half-turned, evidently torn between her dignity and her curiosity. "Come here," Kate said.

Slowly Frances turned and trudged back to Kate's chair. "What do you want?"

"Give me a crayon," Kate said.

Frances started to shake her head. Then she seemed to reconsider, and began rummaging in her crayon box, through all the splendor of gold and silver, copper, violet, aquamarine. She handed Kate a stub of brown.

"Now sit," Kate said. Frances sat.

For the next half hour Frances sat, and Kate sketched her on a piece of notebook paper. At first the stub of crayon and the blue lines were impediments, but gradually Kate lost herself in the drawing, and Frances sat amazingly still.

"That's not very good," Frances said eventually, when she was able to sit no longer. "It doesn't look anything like me."

"I know that," Kate said.

Frances was right, of course. The picture not only didn't look like her, it didn't look like much of anything. The proportions were wrong. The leg that Kate had tried to foreshorten looked like a stump.

"So I'm going to color now," Frances said.

"You do that. But just remember to tell your mother I drew you."

135

Frances gave her a blank look, blanker than ever, and then she went off toward the barn.

Later, when her own mother got back from town, Kate was still studying the drawing. "You wonder what that is?" she said, looking at her mother. "That's a human body."

"I thought maybe it was."

"What's wrong with it? What am I doing?"

Her mother leaned over her shoulder, frowning at the drawing on the notebook page.

"Well, this leg, for instance. The foot looks like it's attached to the knee."

"That's called foreshortening."

Her mother laughed. "It may be that you need to look again." And then she sat down on the grass with the notebook on her lap and drew a little seated figure with one leg extended and foreshortened as Kate had tried to do. "Something like that," she said.

Kate picked up the notebook and looked at the figure her mother had drawn. A person could learn to foreshorten a leg, she thought, to draw a figure that was perfectly adequate. It was the other thing that you couldn't learn, that was simply there, like a present. She knew because she recognized this other thing in her father's work. It was there, whether she liked what he painted or not. And it was there in her picture of the meadow.

Hesitantly Kate put the notebook down on the grass. She had known this other thing was there while she was painting. She had felt it. A present. Something that came uninvited, unlearned. But it was not here. It was not in "Jones Beach."

She looked down at the figure in the notebook. "I see what I should have done with the leg," she said. "Thank you."

"It isn't really very hard," said her mother. "It's the kind of thing you learn to do in art school."

Kate wanted to touch her. Her hand moved, and then she thought, no. Touching was their way of consoling one another.

And so she said, "I've almost finished this paper. Finally. All I need is a kind of summing up. I think what I'm going to do when I finish it is to try to paint a picture of Frances."

"Frances?"

"Why not? I've been painting a little, you know."

"Ian told me."

"*Ian* told you. Why?"

"I think he knew it would please me."

Kate found Mrs. Hilmer in the kitchen, part way into the oven with a steel wool pad. She seemed somehow more approachable this way. "Mrs. Hilmer, I'd like to try doing a painting of Frances," Kate said, addressing Mrs. Hilmer's back.

"You?"

"Yes. I've been painting a little this summer. I used to

137

paint quite a lot." Kate hesitated, studying the wide expanse before her. "Of course, I'd do it for free."

"Well, I should think you *would*," came the reply, echoing out of the cave of the oven. And that was all.

But the next day there was Frances, settled with her crayons under a tree. She was wearing her Light Princess costume, and Kate knew she had come to pose. Kate hadn't meant that they'd start right away. She had wanted to be sure that the paper was finished. But there was Frances.

There were moments when she wondered why she'd ever chosen to do this. It wasn't always pleasant, since Frances remained entirely herself. But Kate kept at it. She worked mornings, trying to get at what it was that was essentially Frances in the crouching figure, crumpling one piece of paper after another. She had decided to do the whole figure, and at a distance, because she knew that she could never do a face that would satisfy either Frances or Mrs. Hilmer. It was hard work.

Sometimes her mother came out into the yard to look at her progress. Sometimes Amanda came. If Amanda was home, she always came, and that was the worst part. She could hardly stand what Kate was doing.

"Nobody has ever painted a picture of me," she said. "In all my whole life."

She didn't say this just once. She stood beside Kate, chewing the end of a lanyard, saying it every few minutes. And the more often she said it, the more important Frances became, smiling in a superior way that Kate finally couldn't tolerate.

"Okay," she said to Amanda, "I'll do you next."

And then she had not one but two pictures to finish in the short time remaining before she went back to school.

18

One day there was a postcard from Ian. It was a picture of the Grand Canyon at sunset—a hideous raspberry-colored sky above pink rocks. No sky or rocks had ever looked like that, Kate thought, examining the photograph. And apparently Ian had known how the picture would strike her, for his message said simply, "You could do better than this."

She used the card as a bookmark, substituting it for the leaves and bits of grass that had marked her place all summer. She thought she would always keep it in the book.

"I had a postcard from Ian," she said to her mother, and her mother, who was doing something with a large piece of salmon, said, "I'm glad."

Her mother was cheerful these days because Kate's father

was painting. The very fact that they all noticed this made Kate realize how long it had been since she had seen him actually at work.

She saw him now, through the screen door, standing at the easel. She tiptoed in with the coffee and the mail so as not to disturb him, put the things down quietly, and glanced briefly at what he was doing.

And then glanced again. It was awful. The red stroke he was layering on with a palette knife was all wrong—a long, red vertical stroke that looked somehow desperate.

"Oh, don't do that," she said, and then clapped her hand over her mouth exactly as she'd seen it done in movies.

He turned to look at her mildly enough. "No?" he said. "Why not?"

"Because," Kate said slowly, "it isn't going to do what you think it will."

"And what is that?"

"Change the picture. I mean, it will change it, but I think it will make it worse."

He looked at the canvas with its irrelevant, angry streak of red. "Worse," he said. "That's an interesting choice of words."

Kate said nothing, hearing what she had already said.

"Do you wonder why I haven't just chucked it out?" he said. "You must have wondered in all this time. Weeks and weeks and nothing happening."

And still Kate said nothing.

"Well, I'll tell you why. I'm having a war with this

painting. It's trying to beat me, and I don't plan to let it."

And then he looked down at the red-smeared palette knife dangling in his hand. "And the other reason," he said more slowly, "is that I have no idea what's coming next."

"Do you usually know?"

"Usually?" He shrugged. "Usually I have enough ideas in my head to last me a year. When I came to this island, I thought I'd never have enough time to paint all the pictures I had in mind. They swarmed in my head."

"And now they don't?"

"And now they don't."

Kate didn't know how to answer him, and yet it seemed to her that she ought to say something, that he was expecting her to. And so she said, "But the exhibit in Berkeley, the retrospective—you must be pleased about that."

"Pleased?" He walked slowly across the room and stood at the long window that looked out across the meadow. "Do you know what a retrospective is, Kate?"

"Of course, I know. It's a great honor."

He stood for a time saying nothing, and then, finally, "You must also know then that most painters aren't offered retrospective exhibits until everyone assumes that their best work is behind them."

Kate could find nothing to reply because, looking at him standing there with the sun from the skylights like a shawl on his shoulders, she saw for the first time that her father had become an old man.

142

She walked up to the house, opened her book, and looked at Ian's postcard. She sat holding it as if it were a kind of rudder steadying her confusion. Old. It had happened without her noticing. And she had a sense of time playing tricks, rushing along while her back was turned.

On the step beside her lay her notebook. The paper was finished. A picture of Frances was almost finished. The summer that had seemed so long had shrunk to almost nothing. Her father was old.

Kate read over the last few sentences of the paper that she had written that morning, hurrying to finish so she could type it. "It is wrong," she had written, "morally, politically, humanly wrong for a ruler to ignore the needs of his people. To use others for his own purposes with no concern for the cost to them is unforgivable. Prospero is guilty of these things."

She had meant to end the paper there, with this indictment, like a trial lawyer summing up her case. But now she hesitated. Looking down over the yellowing grass in the meadow, she sat for a long time before, finally, picking up her pencil.

"And yet at the end of the play," she wrote, "Prospero has become an old man. His magic powers are nearly gone, and then they are gone entirely. In the Epilogue he asks us to set him free. I think Shakespeare means for us to forgive him. I think he means that if we refuse, we will be trapped like Prospero was, on his island."

Kate read this over. In a way, it messed up her conclusion, her neat case. She wasn't even sure it was true. Maybe Shakespeare meant no such thing. But it was what she meant, so she left it.

The young painter who came to dinner to eat the poached salmon was strangely thin and elegant. He might even, Kate thought, be famous. His name sounded vaguely familiar. Certainly he seemed to expect her to know it.

He more lounged than sat in Ian's chair, twirling the stem of his wine glass while her father talked. She resented his being in Ian's chair, which she knew was irrational. She also knew that she didn't care if it was irrational. She wasn't ready to see someone else sitting there, particularly this painter.

She minded his slouch and the way his eyes wandered up and down the table while her father talked. She minded his limp, exhausted voice that made everything he said seem an effort for him. He was bored and that was obvious. It seemed rude to her that he should eat her mother's salmon and drink her father's wine so carelessly, and make so little effort to hide the fact of his boredom.

Her father was excited about the theory he was discussing. His eyes sparked. Kate could feel some of the old, cool, white electricity in the air, but she thought it was lost on this lounging guest.

Because the painter was making her angry, she looked at the painting behind him. She had eaten meals across from it most of her life. It was entirely familiar, but she preferred it to the painter.

She could remember the summer her father had painted it, painting outside for once, beside the house. It was a view of the wall of the house he had painted, the same gray, gentle expanse of shingles on which she had watched the light changing. But there was nothing soft or gentle about her father's view. "Vertical Study" was what he had called it, and that's what it was—one dark vertical stroke thrusting its way up across the deep yellow canvas. It baffled her to think that it was possible for two people to look at the same thing and see it so differently.

If she were going to paint that view, Kate thought, she would retain some part of the wall itself. Color, yes, and light, but also the articulation of the shingles, the intersection of the roof. Hers would be a wall that even Frances Hilmer could look at and name. That was the way she would want to paint it.

"And so you see," her father was saying, "why I have chosen to go the way I have. There are one or two of us who have just kept at our work in our own way all these years, not paying too much attention to trends."

The young painter nodded, tapping his thumbnail on the rim of his wine glass. "I guess that would be considered fairly well out of the mainstream now," he said.

It seemed to Kate that there was a sudden vacuum in the room—two beats of emptiness—and then her father reached out and poured the man more wine. "In some circles, no doubt," he said.

"The whole expressionist thing has gone in another direction."

"Well, there you're using labels," her father said, but his voice sounded quiet to Kate, and tired.

She looked across the table at this inhabitant of Ian's chair. She couldn't stand him. She couldn't stand his long, thin fingers twiddling with his wine glass, or his smooth, conceited face. She couldn't imagine Ian's ever being so rude. Looking at him, *she* felt rude.

She lifted a slice of cucumber on her fork and looked at it critically. "What's this business about 'the mainstream' anyway?" she said. "This business about various movements? What's any of that got to do with painting?"

The man turned and smiled at her, and she could see that he thought she didn't know a damned thing about painting or criticism either. "Well, quite a lot actually," he said.

"No, it hasn't," Kate said quietly, bent now on cutting the cucumber in half. "Painting has to do with knocking yourself out day after day trying to get what you want to down on the canvas. Maybe it works and maybe it doesn't, but every day you try. That's what painting is."

And then she waited for someone to say something. She thought that certainly her mother would rush in to say something polite. But for a minute nobody spoke, and then her father said, "My daughter's right, you know."

146

19

Now the evenings were chilly, and, in the morning, the dew on the grass was cold. Kate began to think about school, and what to take with her and what to leave home.

She had finished a watercolor of Frances that satisfied her at last. She had begun on Amanda. And now Frances was the one standing at her elbow, commenting on every other stroke she painted.

Because the paper was finished, Kate's afternoons were free, and she often spent them with her mother. Sometimes they worked in the garden, but often they simply sat in the sun and talked.

"Frances hates her picture," Kate said.

"Well, Frances isn't a noted critic."

"She doesn't like it that I didn't paint the sequins on her costume."

Her mother laughed.

"I told her to put the sequins in herself," said Kate. "She's the one with the gold and silver crayons."

On another day she said, "You know, it's funny the way things work out. If I hadn't invited Peter Wagner to the spring dance at school, I'd have spent the summer on Long Island. A lot never would have happened."

"Who's Peter Wagner?"

"Just a friend. He gave me mono."

"You've never mentioned him."

"I've never thought about him, except a couple of times when my glands ached."

And on the last afternoon, "I've liked being home. It's been a good thing to be here."

"It's been nice for me to have you here."

"You get lonely, don't you?"

"Sometimes. A little."

She was looking down into the meadow, and Kate, following her gaze, saw that her father was coming slowly up the path from the studio. He sometimes did this now in the late afternoon, coming up to the house in search of her mother. Kate knew that when he reached them there would be no chance to talk, and so she said quickly, "It was you who bought me the paints, wasn't it? You got him to take me with him when he went to the museum Sunday afternoons."

No answer, and he was almost beside them.

"Wasn't it?" Kate said. And then, "I know it was. So, thank you. That's all I wanted to say."

In order to catch a bus that would get her to school by evening, Kate took a midmorning ferry. It was a sunny day, but there was a sharp breeze on the water. A few sailboats were skidding across the Sound, heeling hard in the breeze. The usual ragtag crowd of sea gulls trailed after the boat, and Kate threw them the last bit of the doughnut she'd bought and watched them swarm and jostle to catch it.

They passed the far bell buoy. Kate leaned on the rail, looking back at the island, at the gray shingled houses growing small along the shore, at the pair of lighthouses that marked the island's western points, and at the red clay cliffs just visible in the Indian summer haze.

And then they were too far out from land to mark details. The island floated, drifting in the sunlight, fading into the middle distance as the ferry moved on.

ABOUT THE AUTHOR

Zibby Oneal says, "I grew up in a house full of books, and from an early age I was determined to be a writer. But I grew up in a house that was full of paintings as well, and, though I am no artist, I think in terms of color and composition. All my books have begun with a picture in mind— a character and a place visualized. When I can see these things clearly—almost as if they were a painting on a wall— then I can begin to write about them.

"I began writing for children when my own two were small. My characters aged along with them. Eventually everyone reached adolescence, but my characters remained there, because I found I was deeply interested in exploring this brief time of life, these few years when everything is in the process of becoming what it will be." Ms. Oneal graduated from the University of Michigan, where she now teaches literature and creative writing. She and her husband live in Ann Arbor.

The Language of Goldfish

An ALA Notable Book
An ALA Best Book for Young Adults
A *School Library Journal* Best Book of the Year
A *Booklist* Reviewers' Choice
An ALA *Best of the Best Books, 1970–1982*
A *Booklist* "Contemporary Classic"

"An honest and gripping novel that lingers long in memory."
—ALA *Booklist,* starred review

"A triumphant, highly suggestible book."
—B. Dalton, Bookseller, *Hooked on Books*

"A moving portrait."—*Horn Book*

A Formal Feeling

An ALA Notable Book
An ALA Best Book for Young Adults
A *New York Times* Best Book of the Year
A *Booklist* Reviewers' Choice
Winner of the Christopher Award
An ALA *Best of the Best Books, 1970–1982*
An *American Bookseller* "Pick of the Lists"

"Filled with scenes of great emotional intensity and perception."
—ALA *Booklist,* starred review

"An outstanding book." —*School Library Journal,* starred review

"Beautifully drawn and truly affecting."
—*The New York Times Book Review*